T.L. BODINE

These Kids Are Not Alright

THESE KIDS ARE NOT ALRIGHT

T L BODINE

Contents

Content Warnings   iv

1   Plush   1

2   Feral Children   4

3   More Time   15

4   Cowbirds   20

5   The Toymaker   37

6   Beware the Wolves   46

7   The Twins   56

8   Camp Tailypo   58

9   Not Even Once   76

10 Thoughts and Prayers   82

11 Home for the Holidays   96

12 The Observer Effect   107

13 Sick   124

14 Blackwood   128

15 Transilience   145

Author's Notes   152

Acknowledgments   153

About the Author   154

Content Warnings

This collection includes content that may be disturbing for some audiences, including: child death and endangerment, animal death, and (implied) sexual violence. Reader discretion is advised.

In memory of Eirik.
I think you would have liked this one.

1

Plush

In response to growing demand and technological innovations, PLUSH*CO is proud to announce our newest product offering.

Nearly a decade ago, PLUSH*CO revolutionized the stuffed toy market with our line of *Fur-ever Friends*™ posable animals. Each *Fur-ever Friend*™ is carefully crafted and beautifully realistic in every regard, from the fur texture to the details of the paw pads, nose, eyes, and teeth. Our proprietary stuffing mix replicates the lifelike heft and warmth of a living animal, making every cuddle feel real. The articulated wire armature allows for complete posing flexibility. Original parts are used wherever possible for maximum authenticity.

That attention to detail is the secret of our success. In our modern world, most people are simply too busy to manage the mess and hassle of pet ownership. But at the same time, the need to hold, cherish, love, and cuddle something is hard-coded into our DNA. We have answered the growing demand for realistic stuffed toys that bring the comfort and rewards of pet ownership without the hassle of food costs, vet bills, floor messes, and daily walks.

At the same time, an enduring key to the success of PLUSH*CO has been our partnership with animal shelters across the country. This partnership has helped us in two ways. First, it solved the issue of obtaining quality fur, teeth, claws, and other details. The weight, texture, smell, and color possibilities in synthetic materials simply cannot compete with the real thing, and buyers respond best to the uniqueness and authenticity of our specimens. Our team of FUNgineers combines expertise in taxidermy, animatronics, and toy design to ensure every *Fur-ever Friend*™ is designed with safety and longevity in mind.

The second benefit has been to our animal control partners.

Demand for low-maintenance, obedient, cuddly friends coupled with a growing lack of free time and energy among a busy workforce had created a massive over-supply of dogs, cats, and pocket pets. Animals were being abandoned and surrendered at levels far exceeding adoption rates, creating a problem with shelter over-crowding and euthanasia.

By generously supplying euthanized specimens, shelters were able to keep their residency numbers low. And, thanks to the runaway success of *Fur-ever Friends*™, we are able to pay a premium for these unique specimens, vastly boosting the funding of these historically under-served public services.

Today, nearly a decade into our *Fur-ever Friends*™ experiment, we are happy to say that animal shelters across the country are empty! More than that, for the first time in our nation's history, the streets are totally clear of stray cats, free-roaming dogs, pesky squirrels and raccoons, and other nuisances. In fact, take a look around: when was the last time you've seen a live animal?

But times change, and it is imperative that we keep up with shifting demand and the reality of a dwindling supply. The stuffed toy market for cuddly pets is becoming saturated. At the same time, there is increasing consumer demand for a product that serves the human caregiving instinct at a deeper, more primal level. Career and economic realities have made parenthood increasingly out of reach for many hard-working Americans, while putting tremendous pressure on others who lack the time, money, health, or energy to care for their existing children. We here at PLUSH*CO have just the solution.

Coming this fall: *Forever Baby™*.

You've never seen a baby doll this realistic before.*

*Subject to availability. All models are hand-grown. Please allow up to 9 months for production.

2

Feral Children

Three children was far too many. Landlords wouldn't allow three children. And though their parents tried their best to hide them, Hans and Greta were eventually found out during a surprise inspection—and with the eviction notice pinned to the door, what else were their parents meant to do?

"We can keep two," their mother said, still hopeful.

"But which?" Their father dragged a hand over his eyes. "It would be cruel to separate them. At least this way they'll have each other. And we could try again, down the line. What are the chances of having twins a second time?"

"We could keep them both…" their mother started.

"Absolutely not. Jack was here first, it would be unfair to him to throw him out."

"But he's nearly sixteen…"

"Nobody wants a child his age. He'd surely die on his own. But the twins are so young and cute. They'll find a home right away–I promise."

He took his wife in his arms and kissed her forehead, giving her shoulders a reassuring squeeze.

~*~

"What do you mean, you're not taking surrenders right now?" Color bloomed in their father's face, his voice lifting. The twins cowered behind him.

"Just what I said, sir. I'm sorry. But we're at capacity."

Beyond the reception area, out in the housing space, there were distant sounds of yelling, laughter and crying and some noise that sounded like both at the same time. It made the hair on Greta's arms stand upright and her skin tingle. But her brother wrapped an arm around her, trying to stand tall.

"Well, I can't take them back to my house!" Father yelled, loud enough that an employee stopped walking past in order to turn and gawk. "Not unless you want our whole family turned out in the street."

"I'm sorry," the receptionist repeated. "But as a no-kill facility, we have hard limits on our capacity. We can't take any more children until some are adopted or a foster opens up. That's just how it has to be."

"What about the city pound?"

The receptionist frowned. "They can't turn you away," she admitted. "But I have to warn you...their funding is even worse than ours. I promise you they're at capacity, too. Giving them your children is pretty much signing a death sentence for a different kid. Have you tried asking a relative, or posting an ad online?"

"Have I tried....? Jesus. What do you think I am? Did you think this was my first choice? Like I'm some idiot who didn't...look. I need this dealt with tonight, before my landlord comes back and inspects the house again."

He turned and gripped each twin by the shoulder, steering

them back out the door.

~*~

It was near dark by the time their father pulled off the road. The city was far behind them; now they looked out over a wooded area. The trees were thick and close, and it was dark between their trunks.

Greta slumped down in her seat, making a quiet, frightened noise.

"Get out," their father said, putting a threat in his voice.

His hand curled into a fist, as if preparing to strike them.

"Go on. Get out of here."

Jack, in the front seat, kept his gaze averted, staring out the window, his jaw wobbling a little like he was trying not to cry.

Hans looked between his father and brother, then let out a breath. He pushed open his door and tugged at Greta's wrist. "It's all right," he whispered. "I'll take care of you. Let's just go."

Greta eyed her twin skeptically but followed him anyway. She murmured a farewell to Jack, who had always been kind to her, but she wouldn't meet her father's eyes. They closed the car door behind them and stepped down onto the grassy shoulder, hand-in-hand.

At first, the car didn't move, and they could make out their father's face through the glass, the way his gaze followed them in the rear-view mirror. A slight downturn of his lips, a twitch in his cheek—but the expression quickly passed, and his gaze flicked away.

A moment later, the car's tires crunched over gravel, and it was replaced just by the glow of taillights in a cloud of dusty exhaust.

"We'd better go," Hans said, squeezing his sister's hand.

"Do you know where we're going?" Greta asked.

He shook his head. "No. But maybe if we walk into the trees, we'll find something. It can be like an adventure."

Greta was not feeling very adventurous. She was feeling sad and hungry. But she didn't have any better ideas, so she walked into the woods with Hans, and they wandered through trees in the ever-darkening forest.

After a while, when it was full dark and the woods were coming alive with night sounds, Greta spotted an orange glow ahead. She elbowed her brother.

"Look!"

"What is that?"

"I don't know. But it's something different than cold and dark."

The twins crossed the forested lot, winding between the trees, until they came up on a fence. Over the top, they could see the roof of a house, with light in the windows. There was a gap in the fence, big enough for a child to squeeze through, and Hans stepped forward first to investigate.

"Greta, come look!"

Laid out on the back porch was a table piled high with food: a tray of sandwiches and liter bottles of soda, a plate of cookies.

But more amazing: they were not alone. Crowded around the table were many other children, some of them much older than the twins, and some much younger. The older ones were dressed in filthy rags and had ragged, broken-off nails. Some had scars on their arms and faces, wounds like bites and scratches. The youngest kids were naked, crouching like wild things over food they'd pulled from the table. They scattered fearfully when Hans and Greta approached.

One of the bigger boys was missing an eye, and when he turned to look at them, they could see the way his eyelid crumpled in over the empty socket, weeping clear fluid at the edge.

"Do you live here?" Hans asked, hesitantly stepping forward.

"I live wherever I want," the one-eyed boy said. He looked older than Jack, practically a grown-up, and he towered over most of the others who crowded around him on either side.

"What is this place?"

The one-eyed boy shrugged. "It's free food. Don't ask questions."

Greta thought that was a very sensible plan. She took two sandwiches for herself and slipped handfuls of cookies into her pockets. She tried to take one of the bottles of soda, but an older girl—a teenager, clutching a little naked baby to her chest—bared her teeth and made a low warning noise, so Greta backed away with what she had.

~*~

Hans and Greta spent several weeks in the woods, where they learned the rules that governed the other children.

Bordering the small patch of woods they had been abandoned in was a subdivision. The house with the gap in its fence belonged to a family of softhearted people who usually left food out for the children. Sometimes they forgot, or were too busy to bother, and so the children went hungry or else hunted the small creatures that lived in the woods—mice and birds and lizards.

When they weren't eating, the children retreated into the safety of the treeline, sleeping by themselves or breaking off into little groups. The children who were no longer really children would start their own families; that was why there were no clothes for the littlest ones.

"Do you ever go inside?" Hans once asked.

"Sometimes, when one of us gets hurt," the one-eyed boy, whose name was Tom, explained, "the family takes them to a doctor. But they don't keep any of the children. Most of us are too wild to be kept, anyway."

"What about the babies?" Greta asked.

Tom shrugged. "They're the most wild of all. They've never known anything different."

"What about you, Tom? Did you used to have a house and parents like us?"

"I don't remember anymore," Tom said, in a way that made Greta realize he didn't want to answer any more questions, so she stopped asking them.

For the first few nights, the twins entertained the idea that their parents might miss them—that they might come out and look for them, or change their minds about abandoning them. But when no one came for them after a week, they abandoned that thought and learned to live like the other stray children, their hair growing shaggy, their bodies dirty. They learned to scrap and claw and bite when others got too close or threatened them; they learned to defend their best sleeping places and their food.

One day, Tom did not join them at the table. They found his body later, by the road, half-curled in on itself, parts of him missing or smeared on the pavement. At night, the forest filled with high, keening noises: girls crying, babies wailing.

"I think Tom was the boss," Greta said. "Like the dad. I think he took care of them."

"Then someone else will have to. I think I have an idea."

~*~

The Bruins were a proper family: A mother and a father and a son just a little bit younger than Hans and Greta. They lived in a proper house, with two bedrooms and a guest room that they kept for company. They were clean, well-mannered people with respectable jobs, and the little boy went to a good school. The only problem was their affection for strays.

"Feeding them just attracts more of them," the man across the street tried to explain once, when he and Mr. Bruins both happened to be outside watering their lawns at the same time. "And then they stay and get into fights and some of them breed, which just makes everything worse."

"I suppose you're right," Mr. Bruins admitted. "It's just my wife has such a kind heart, and she can't stand to think of them starving. We'd take them all in ourselves if we could, you know. They're just…"

And there he trailed off with a sort of sheepish half-shrug, and he went back inside when the lawn was finished, and his neighbor went back inside and thought about how much he hated his neighbor for feeding the feral children, and how the hoards of them were driving down the property value for the whole block.

Because the Bruins were a proper family, they were all gone away at work or school during the day, leaving the house quite empty.

When the sun was out, and the other children were mostly hidden away to sleep in the shade during the hottest hours, Hans and Greta slipped through the hole in the fence and came up to the back door. The porch door was locked, but they found an open window in the kitchen. Greta was able to climb inside by standing on her brother's shoulders, and then she crouched on the counter by the sink and bent down to take his hands, hauling him up.

She slithered down onto the floor, exhausted with the effort, and he sprawled on the counter top, panting, before they both could collect themselves. Greta stood up and Hans climbed down and both of them washed their hands and faces in the kitchen sink and drank long and deep from the tap.

Then they began to explore the house.

They found a lot of food, even more than they ever saw in their own home. Mr. Bruins liked protein bars and whey powders, which the twins found too bitter, and Mrs. Bruins liked big salads with lots of vegetables, which the twins didn't think were very filling. But Junior Bruins liked peanut butter sandwiches and individually wrapped cheese slices, which they thought were perfect. They made sandwiches for now and for later, and stuffed the cheese in their pockets out of habit.

They explored the rest of the house, taking their time to look at everything. There was a big, firm couch made of the kind of leather that sticks when you sit on it, and the television was the kind with Netflix right there on the remote. Each Bruins family member had their own account, and the twins checked out each one. At home, they'd only ever gotten to watch whatever their parents put on the television for them.

Mr. Bruins liked nature documentaries and shows about fixing cars, which were pretty boring.

Mrs. Bruins liked romantic movies and shows with Korean actors, but the twins didn't like having to read the subtitles.

But they liked the cartoons that Junior Bruins preferred well enough, and they watched a few different ones together, eating more of the sandwiches they'd made.

The television made them sleepy, so they left the living room and went down the hall. The guest bedroom was too cold and empty; there was even dust on the windowsill and the bed wasn't made up properly. The master bedroom was too dark and smelly. The grown-ups were slobs with their laundry, leaving it out all over the floor, and there was a dank, sweaty smell hanging over the bed. Greta and Hans wrinkled their noses and left.

Junior Bruins had a nice room, though.

He even had bunk beds, so his friends could sleep over.

Hans took the top bed, and Greta took the bottom, and they stretched out luxuriously beneath the blankets and fell asleep, warm and comfortable and snug.

~*~

That afternoon, Junior Bruins saw two strange children sleeping in his bed and he screamed.

His parents, already on high alert after finding the television on, remnants of protein powder and empty peanut butter jars scattered on the kitchen counter, sprinted into the room to see what was the matter. Mr. Bruins pushed his wife and son behind him, trying to shield them with his body as he faced down the intruders.

Hans and Greta stirred awake, disoriented.

Greta pulled the blankets up around her chin, protectively, but Hans saw all too easily where this was headed. From the top bunk, it was easy to see the look in the man's eye, his telegraphed meaning. And now that he'd gotten proper rest in a proper bed, Hans had no intention at all of ever returning to the damp and dirty woods.

"Get Junior out of here!" Mr. Bruins yelled. "And call child services! Or animal control! The police! Anyone!"

Feeding feral children was one matter. Having one in your house, spitting and angry, was something quite different.

Mr. Bruins looked around the room for some kind of weapon, something he could use to defend himself. His gaze landed on a baseball bat. He reached for it, but not in time.

Hans, his body coiled like a spring, leaped from the top bunk and slammed into the man, his fingernails clawing at his face, his feet wrapping around his middle, squeezing for purchase. Mr. Bruins, caught off guard by the weight, staggered backward, pinwheeling his arms for balance. Mrs. Bruins, still in the doorway, screamed.

Greta jumped forward, understanding now what had to be done. She slammed into the man's knees, and they bent backwards with the force of the impact, the joints reversing with an audible crunch.

Mr. Bruins cried out in pain and surprise, crumpling on ruined legs. Hans bit his ear for good measure, snapping his sharp little teeth through the soft flap of skin and cartilage. He spat out the earlobe as he rode Mr. Bruins to the floor, pinning his body over the man's chest, and looked up at Mrs. Bruins and her son in the hall. His eyes caught the light; when he bared his teeth, they glistened crimson.

Mrs. Bruins tried to run, then, but Greta was very fast, and she didn't get very far.

~*~

For a long time, the Bruins had fed the strays, and nobody in the neighborhood liked it, but they put up with it because they wanted to be neighborly. But this was just too much.

Attracted from years of indulgence and free food, the strays had proliferated in the neighborhood—and now they were running wild all over, scratching up lawns and clawing at doorways, snatching up food left on patio grills and stealing groceries from parked cars. They were a relentless nuisance, and they seemed to be pouring into the neighborhood from the Bruins house.

The city deployed its vans to round up the strays as they found them. They got the paperwork they needed to enter the house. One investigator pushed open the door, and his partner gasped and started to cough, her eyes watering immediately with the stench—the scent of feces and blood and rot, and another smell, earthy like soft dirt.

"Go call for backup," the female officer said. "This is a mess."

Her partner was more than happy to retreat.

Covering her mouth, the investigator stepped inside and then froze, seeing movement in the corner of her eye. She turned slowly to look and locked eyes with a little girl, hair tangled around her face, eyes wide and rimmed in white.

She gripped something gray-white in her teeth. Flesh covered one end: a wrist and a hand missing some of its fingers.

The investigator was too stunned in her horror at the girl to notice the other twin who had slipped around behind.

How lucky, Hans thought. They had a lot of work to do, all this luring and catching.

There were many children in this neighborhood that needed to be fed.

3

More Time

The dead are restless in our village.

It has been this way since the time of the wasting sickness. People will fall ill with fever. By the second day, their bodies begin to contort and spasm, their muscles tightening, their joints bending and popping in the wrong ways. By the third day, they go stiff, their lips pulled back in a grimace, only their eyes moving.

By the fourth day, they will die.

They must be buried before sunrise. That is the custom. They must be buried before the movement returns to their bodies, before they rise with awful hunger.

~*~

We dug the grave beneath the tree on the hill overlooking our farm. There are no graveyards anymore. We fear to let the dead speak to one another in their language of low moans. We worry at what will happen if they rise together, in numbers great enough to overwhelm us.

We learned that lesson hard, the first time. We lost many families that day.

Now we bury our dead beneath the trees so that their voices might be heard by the roots, so they might speak to us in the whisper of leaves.

We held his funeral in the usual way, with dancing and song and offerings laid around the fresh-dug earth. It lasted through the night and into the dawn, as these things always do. And then the mourners left, the last stragglers giving their farewells and condolences, and I lay sprawled and weeping over the soft, upturned earth and watered it with my tears.

The grief was a vast, growing emptiness. It bloomed inside me, something ravenous, like a kind of wasting sickness in its own way. It created a nest in me, a trembling place carved by shock and pain and the loss of something precious, irreplaceable.

By the third day, the pain of it was unbearable. The agony was blinding in its intensity.

Tobias. My son. My baby. I needed to see him. I needed to hold him one more time.

~*~

I made my way out to the field, stopping beneath the spread-out and skeletal branches of the ancient elm. I began to dig.

Excavating the grave took hours, every shovelful of dirt sending a searing rip of pain between my shoulders, down my spine. But I did not stop until I saw him, wrapped as he was in his shroud, looking pale and peaceful in his slumber. The days had not touched his body beneath the earth. He was beautiful. My baby boy.

I held him to my breast and wept, and he curled a tiny fist

into the fabric of my shirt and drew himself closer. I brought him home, and he took his place in bed between myself and my husband. We alternated in dozing and merely gazing at him in wonderment, smoothing back his soft blond hair, running gentle fingers over the unblemished skin. It was like bringing him home for the first time, again. The wonder. The miracle of his life.

We thought that if we kept him close between us, warmth might return to his body.

We thought, with enough time, he might become our son again.

~*~

Tobias was not the same after I pulled him from the earth.

He was cold and quiet. His face held some reptilian calculation, some stony emptiness, that does not belong to a child. There was a stranger there, behind his milky eyes.

When he walked, it was with a staggering gait, drunken or uncertain about how to place each foot.

His mouth sometimes would open and close, open and close, like an infant seeking a breast, tiny teeth chattering against each other as he peered vacantly, fish-eyed, around the room.

The sickness wore his body like a costume.

He did not do much. He did not laugh or cry or sing. He did not reach for his toys or smile when he saw us. He only sat, and snapped at the air with his baby teeth. If stray flesh crossed his path—a careless hand, a bare throat—he snapped and bit, but his tiny teeth lacked the strength to cut through flesh.

"We are safe from the sickness," my husband said, trying to find the blessing in it. "He will not make us one of them."

He was right, but it brought me little comfort. The longer Tobias stayed with us, the more I wished we had left him in the earth.

~*~

On the third day, he began to smell. The odor clung to him, the sick-sweet stench of infection and the sulfurous reek of Hell.

~*~

On the fourth day, fluids began to ooze from him, dark and thick and staining. They trailed the floors and sank into the mattress, a syrup that smelled of decay.

~*~

On the fifth day, I returned him to his grave.

He gazed up at me, too weak to lift an arm in protest as I carried his body back across the fields. He did not cry out. He had not spoken since the sickness took hold. None of them do; theirs is not a language of words.

The hole yawned empty before me. I wrapped his body and laid him inside, and he flinched away and crawled into the corner of the grave, body curling in on itself like a garden slug, damp and boneless. He gazed up through pale lashes, eyes now grown impossibly large, wide deep pools set over the bony hollows of his pale cheeks.

His mouth worked, click-click-click, teeth against teeth but voiceless.

He stared after me as each shovelful of dirt rained down upon him. I smoothed over the surface and laid down the heavy stone that would seal the loose-packed dirt and leaned against my shovel, my body singing with pain.

Below, deep below, the earth moaned, dirt shifting with the plaintive efforts of tiny fists.

4

Cowbirds

The clinics were still open when the Cowbirds arrived. The first time I saw one was on the ultrasound monitor for a young couple who came in that day. Of course, I didn't know at the time what I was looking at; none of us understood, at first.

Nothing about the couple was particularly abnormal. I introduced myself and explained what we'd be doing that day, and the father-to-be—husband, boyfriend, I'm not sure which—eyed me with the kind of skepticism I'm used to in the field.

A female abortion doctor catches people by surprise. That I was visibly pregnant turned heads, too. Everyone always assumes that you specialize in family planning because you hate babies, when the truth is—at least for me—the exact opposite. I love babies. I love them so much that I think every single one of them deserves to be wanted and loved and cared for by people who are excited for the job.

And to make that happen, would-be parents need to have every option available.

"This will be a bit cold, but it won't hurt," I reassured the woman, pulling on a pair of nitrile gloves. I smeared the ultrasound gel on her belly, applied the wand. "Let's take a look."

On the monitor: Two fetuses, their slender little bean-shaped bodies curved against one another, nestled snug as kittens. Eyes peacefully closed, hearts steadily beating.

The father looked suddenly ashen, his gaze fixed on the monitor.

I caught the look in his eye, glanced between them. Tried to guess at what had caused the sudden shift in atmosphere in the room. "Did you know you were having twins?"

"No," the mother said. "No one ever said...before..."

"It happens," I reassured them. "Sometimes we don't always see both right away. It can be hard to tell at first."

We talked about their options and what they wanted to do, and I explained the prenatal care we offered if they chose to proceed with the pregnancy. I wish I could say that I knew, then, that something unusual had occurred. That I somehow predicted what would happen. But I thought nothing of it until the next patient came and presented with the same scenario: two heartbeats where there had only ever been one.

In the weeks that followed, we started to see the cases tick up. Normally, twins are a rarity—one pregnancy in 250 or so. But we started seeing them a few times a week, then daily. Multiple times a day, until more people were coming in with twin pregnancies than without, and they were always surprised to find that second fetus. Some of them had been pregnant for months with no sign of a twin when a second heartbeat suddenly appeared.

When I went in for my own prenatal exam, I was uneasy, but not surprised, when they found the hidden twin.

~*~

I don't know who first started calling them Cowbirds. In nature, the brown-headed cowbird is a brood parasite, laying its eggs in the nest of a smaller songbird. The much smaller bird ends up raising a fledgling five times its size, the implanted youngster out-competing the natural-born young songbirds.

Before we called them Cowbirds, we came up with more generous names: developmentally accelerated twin; thriving twin; Machiavellian twin.

Sometimes in fetal development, an identical twin will absorb the other, cells folding over and reclaiming a fetus that has stopped growing. Once or twice in a career, you might see it happen. They're called parasitic twins—one host body born with extra parts. Sometimes, too, a fetus dies in utero. When the tissues fall apart, reabsorbed into the mother's body, we call it a vanishing twin.

What we saw with the Cowbirds, these Machiavellian twins, was the opposite of that. Not a vanishing twin, but an appearing one. Two fetuses growing in tandem at first, but one pulling ahead. Growing bigger, stronger. As if it were older than its womb-mate, or as if it were developing on a different timeline entirely.

At first, we assumed it was some kind of delayed fertilization. That the second twin was indeed younger than the initial pregnancy.

But we realized that wasn't the case. The second twin, the one who seemed to appear from nowhere partway into a pregnancy— that was the one that was growing faster. That was the thriving twin.

~*~

No one gets abortions anymore.

In the beginning, we saw an uptick. People daunted by the prospect of supporting two new lives when they'd only expected one. People frightened of these Machiavellian twins, these Cowbirds, who grew so fast, who could not be explained. They saw the reports on the news, the think pieces and speculation, and did not want to be a part of this moment of history. Did not want to be the experimental first wave of an uncertain future.

And so at first we were booked, our appointment ledger filled up.

But things kept going wrong with the procedures. There has always been a measure of risk, a handful of dangerous or deadly complications, but their prevalence increased by a terrible magnitude.

Spontaneous hemorrhaging. Perforations. Infection.

Women left barren. Women left dead.

Lawsuits closed many of the clinics. Others followed under their own power, or spurred along by government mandates. By the time I would have been preparing for maternity leave, there was no job for me to come back to.

~*~

In nature, the real cowbirds keep an eye on the nests where they've planted their eggs. If a wren or robin or chickadee spots the intrusive egg and removes it—pecks it to pieces, kicks it out to smash on the ground below—the cowbird retaliates by returning to the nest and destroying it.

The songbird faces a choice: Destroy the egg and risk losing everything, or leave the egg, incubate it, hatch it, tend to the young, raise the monstrous hatchling and hope that it leaves a little for the others. Raise the outsider's progeny and hope that some of yours survive.

If birds are even capable of such calculus, of course. Maybe birds act on instinct and don't think through these decisions at all. But people do.

~*~

I saw a Cowbird baby for the first time at the grocery store a few days before I was due to deliver. By then, the earliest wave of double births had begun. The oldest twins might be a month or two old by then. I would have guessed that's how old this one was, but the baby was huge.

Its pudgy body was stuffed into a car seat that could barely contain it, the shopping cart nearly tipping with the weight of the seat laid over top. Arms and legs jutted out at awkward angles, waving uselessly—a beetle on its back. The face was wrong, too, somehow, lacking some essential human element. Like a latex mask pulled on and fitted poorly, the eye-holes lopsided, the nose partly caved in, the skin texture too rubbery.

I've seen deformities before, and they do not frighten or repulse me. But this was something different. It looked like something else was moving under its skin. Like the human form was a cocoon, and the thing inside was still taking shape, writhing and rippling and waiting to be born.

The mother caught me watching and started to turn away, defensive. But her gaze dropped to my belly, swollen now beyond the point of containment, a bare sliver of skin peeking out between the hem of my shirt and the top of the not-generous-enough maternity pants.

She offered me a sad, sympathetic smile before walking away.

~*~

"Have you ever done an autopsy on one?"

I shook my head, arm curled protectively around my belly. Talking about fetal autopsies was not my first choice of conversation topic, days before my babies were due, but Rodney was a forensic pathologist and didn't always think about work and life bleeding into one another. When we met in med school, I'd found that kind of passion alluring. It was in my top five reasons I fell in love.

As our first pregnancy neared its conclusion, though, he'd started showing nerves. Started drinking more, too, until a night didn't pass without a beer in hand. He threw himself into his work to settle his anxiety about our future, but it only managed to make him more frightened of what might come next.

"It's wild. I don't know how to explain it." He stared down at his beer bottle, frowning. "Have you ever seen the inside of a butterfly chrysalis? The caterpillar goes in there, but it doesn't just start sprouting wings and legs. It...dissolves. It's all just goo inside. Like cutting open one of those cream-filled eggs at Easter."

I thought about what we'd seen at the clinic, when we were still performing abortions. The remains from most termination procedures are nothing a layperson would be able to easily identify. But what we had seen was abnormal—a mess of tissue with too many pieces, parts we couldn't recognize.

I shuddered, no longer hungry for my dinner.

I went into labor that night.

~*~

We named them Casey and Paul, because Rodney said Castor and Pollux would get both of them bullied too much. He was probably right, although we'd never know. Casey survived only five weeks.

He wasn't the only one. Infant mortality rose that year, nationwide.

Not counting the spontaneous and planned abortions—the pregnancies terminated on purpose, and those that ended on their own—and not counting the stillbirths, the non-thriving twins born shriveled and underdeveloped, mummified after dying in the womb, or else asphyxiated in birthing injuries. Even putting all those numbers aside, more babies died that first year than any time in a century.

"Don't let your infants sleep in the same crib," the PSAs began to warn, when we all finally caught on to what was happening. When it was too late for most of us. "Keep your twins separated when not under your direct supervision."

I'll never forget waking that morning, an early pre-dawn feeding, to hear the sound of just one baby crying. Paul's loud, keening wail—he'd always been the louder twin, the better nurser, the faster grower. When I turned on the light I saw Casey, blue-gray and stiffening. Smashed against the crib bumper, smothered. And beside him, kicking his feet, waving his arms, nearly doubled in size overnight, was Paul. He looked up at me and smiled a wide, toothless smile.

~*~

An essential part of brood parasitism: The cowbird egg incubates faster and hatches sooner than the other eggs in the nest. The fledgling grows bigger. By being stronger, crying louder, shoving its nest-mates out of the nest, it ensures its own survival.

~*~

"Tonight at 7: Cowbirds. Where do they come from, and what do they want? We'll talk to our nation's top scientists and anthropologists as we strive to uncover answers to the question on everybody's mind."

The news played its cheery jingle. It rattled off a few more headlines and features for the evening, but I tuned them out. I was engrossed in my cooking, dinner coming together from rogue ingredients found at the back of a pantry shelf. Money was tight after the clinic closed down, tighter after Casey died and Rodney told me he couldn't do it anymore.

"It's me or that...that thing," he told me, the night we finally fell apart.

"That thing is..." I was going to say our son, but we both knew that wasn't really true. He wasn't born of our union, did not carry our genes. But he had been a part of me, once, had grown inside me. And he was, in his own monstrous way—enormous, deformed, screaming —helpless. He smiled when he looked up at me, trusting and wide-eyed. He needed to be fed and changed and clothed and have his sparse, thin hairs carefully brushed. He was not mine, but he was my responsibility.

So instead I said, "He's just a baby. Whatever he is. He didn't ask to be like this."

That wasn't a good enough answer for Rodney, and I couldn't really blame him—but at the same time I did, because then it was just the two of us, me wasting away while Paul grew bigger and bigger, always hungry. What else was I supposed to do? I had lost one child already, and Paul needed me. Hurting him wouldn't have brought Casey back, but it would have made me a monster.

Didn't Rodney see that by blaming a baby, he was really just blaming me?

"The first question I think we need to ask ourselves," someone on the TV was saying, "is where are the adults? No one has ever seen a fully-grown Cowbird. We don't know how big they'll get, or the trajectory of their development. But we also don't know where they came from. How they were implanted in the human hosts."

"You're talking as if they are confirmed to be inhuman," the host said. "Do you reject, then, the hypothesis that this is a birth defect, genetic anomaly, or—some would go so far as to say—the next phase of human evolution?"

"There is no evidence that the Cowbirds are human."

When did they show up? How long have they been here? What do they want from us?

Those are the questions that showed up on the news every day, that the scientists and policymakers and pundits would all argue about in primetime. No one could seem to agree on anything. Maybe that uncertainty was good for ratings.

"Aliens. Mark my word on this. They're aliens." A different speaker. Another interview, another day; I could tell because the host's hairstyle had changed. "World-conquering invaders. I bet they come to a planet, seed it with their spawn, then come back later to claim the ruins. This is the beginning of the end for the human race, I'm calling it now. So get your affairs in order."

A commercial break. A diaper company, now offering extra-

extra large sizes, "to fit your growing family." At least the capitalist engine keeps turning; there's some comfort in knowing a few things always stay the same. The next commercial was for an attorney's office, a class-action lawsuit notice against an emergency contraception manufacturer. "If you or a loved one used the product in the last 26 months and suffered bleeding, infertility or death, contact us today. You may be entitled to compensation!"

Back to the show. I divided the food out into two plates. A small portion on my dinner plate, a larger, heaping portion spread out across a tray to cool for Paul. He liked it that way, so he could eat with his hands, bury his face in sauce and noodles. I set it in front of him on the coffee table. He'd gotten too big for the high chair, so I just let him sit on the floor, propping himself up on the table edge. His eyes were half-lidded slits, the eyeballs drawn back into the sockets, an expression I'd grown to recognize as contentment. He scooped food into his mouth with pudgy, uncoordinated hands and I turned up the volume on the TV to drown out his wet, throaty smacking.

"I think we need to consider that they've always been here, hidden among us. We have a folk tradition of changelings — faeries who would swap human children for their own, leaving behind miserable, inhuman infants. There may be more to those old stories than we originally thought."

"You're saying this is not the first time something like this has ever happened?"

"That's exactly what I'm saying. Maybe the Cowbirds, or whatever they really are...maybe they live a lot longer than we do. Maybe their reproductive cycle is out of sync with ours, operating at a scale so much larger than we expect. Centuries. Millennia. Like cicadas, emerging at long intervals. They lay dormant for years, then come out in huge numbers. I think it's possible that what we're currently seeing is a swarm."

~*~

There was a real town of Hamelin, like in the story. I don't know whether the part about the rats was true, or if there was ever a piper who led them all away. Probably the children all died of sickness or were conscripted into an army to fight some colonizer's war. But history agrees that all the children of Hamelin went missing—a stolen generation.

We have a stolen generation now, too.

Although I guess, in a way, I've made myself the piper.

~*~

The nursery room was at the back of my client's house. The walls had been painted yellow. Under different lighting, they might have been cheerful, but with the curtains drawn the lamplight cast the room in a sickly, claustrophobic hue. Like being inside an egg.

Or maybe the room just felt claustrophobic because the child inside was so large.

At first glance, you might not notice anything unusual about the baby, aside from the size. Seated, it was nearly at eye-level with me, its pudgy body twice as wide, its grotesquely broad head nodding with the effort of holding up the weight.

"How old did you say it was?"

"Two years."

"Any other children?"

"The other twin. Living with their mother." The pain in his

voice was evident. It strained at his throat. "I don't...I don't want to hurt him. I just can't do this anymore. You understand, right?"

"I do." More than he'd know. He was lucky to have the biological twin—not many of us could boast that two years into this Cowbird pandemic—but I didn't tell him that. There was no point in exacerbating his guilt.

The Cowbird didn't look up when I entered the room. It held a toy car in each hand, smashing them together, and the clatter of plastic-on-plastic drowned out my approach. The closer I got, the more strangeness was evident in its body—strangeness I've seen at home, in Paul, and in other Cowbirds I've met.

They grow fast and they grow big, these Cowbirds, but they never develop. Two years later, they're the size of grown men but they still look like babies.

Looking at him, this monstrous child, cross-legged on the floor, I felt something swoop in my chest. Not love, but not exactly pity or revulsion, either. He looked just like Paul, just like the others. There were minute variations in skin tone and features, modifications to their camouflaged disguises to help them fit in with their host families. But they all looked more similar than different, stamped from the same basic mold. The closer you looked, the less human they appeared.

"What did you do?" the father asked from the doorway, too nervous to step inside. "Before this, I mean."

I unfolded the hand-cart, the specialized carrier I'd started using for this work. "Abortion doctor."

He barked out a dry, humorless laugh.

~*~

I never intended to become this person. I fell into it by accident. I'd been sitting on a park bench, watching Paul crawl around in the grass, a fat happy slug at my feet. Another mother had her Cowbird at the playground. It was stuffed into a dress, all ruffles and lace, as if the frills could hide the misshapen dough quality of the child's body. The woman was trying to get the girl to stand up, to walk, but the girl remained stubbornly seated, a fistful of dirt in each hand. She watched her mother with blank, dark eyes, expressionless as she shoved the dirt into her mouth.

Something about this action broke the mother. She made a guttural, frustrated nose and slapped the child across the face, hard. The skin rippled on impact, waves moving through like jello. She yanked her arm back for another blow.

I'm sure it was a mounting rage, the culmination of a million tiny horrors. I don't know her story, and never asked it, but I'm sure she was hurting. All of us were, in the Cowbird years.

But in that moment, all I knew was she was hurting the child, and I couldn't stand to watch so I launched myself from the bench and thrust my body between her fists and the quivering infant. The Cowbird came up to my waist, just a bit smaller than Paul, and she inclined her head to regard me with a cool, vacant curiosity, eyes wide and dark mouth yawning open.

I caught the mother's wrist in my hand and our eyes met over the Cowbird's broad, bald head and she fell back from me, frustrated tears springing to her eyes. She held up her hands.

"I can't. I can't do this anymore. Please get her away from me. Make it go away. Do something."

I tried to talk her out of it, but I couldn't make her listen. She walked away from us both, not turning to look, and disappeared into the parking lot before I could stop her.

I took the little girl home. She and Paul barely fit, squeezed together in the back seat, her slumping sideways without a booster to hold her upright. I called the police, then child services, to ask what I should do.

"They're not children," they told me. "Try animal control."

I named the girl Artemis.

The next day, I put up an ad for my new business. The money parents gave me to relieve them of their burden, I mostly spent on food and clothing for the children.

Cowbirds are always hungry. Always growing.

~*~

More than two years had passed since the beginning of the twin-birth pandemic, and I had a half-dozen Cowbirds living with me in my home. Not the family I'd imagined for myself, but the one I had. There was never enough food. There was rarely enough sleep. They cried at all hours, one waking the next. But they smiled, too, and cooed, and played with their toes, and even though I worried how big they'd get—Paul was the biggest, towering over me now, barely able to squeeze through the doorframe—I'd made peace with knowing they wouldn't grow up like normal children.

A noise roused me from sleep, and I jolted awake, listening for the cry so I could pinpoint which room needed the attention. But no one was crying. The house was quiet, save for whatever had woken me, and that uncharacteristic silence made me frown.

I climbed out of bed and padded down the hall, opening each door as I went.

All the beds were empty.

Cold seized my veins, my stomach clenching. At the end of the hall, past the kitchen, I could make out the rectangle of the wide-open door. Beyond that, a fat gibbous moon hung silver in the black sky, low enough to the horizon to nearly fill the frame. Something crawled through the door, squeezing with effort outside, and I followed.

They had assembled outside, all six of them—man-sized babies in oversized footy pajamas, crawling on grass-stained knees or standing, wobbly, flabby faces turned toward the moon. They did not cry, but they made some other kind of noise, a low throaty hum that did not come from their mouths.

"Kids," I said. "Hey. Come on. Let's go back inside. It's cold out."

They did not turn to look at me. I was afraid to come closer. They'd formed a circle, all of them standing now, their bodies swaying in time to that strange and awful hum. They were too big to muscle back inside. I might be able to corral one of them, but not all, and I worried what might happen if I came close. Imagined all too clearly how easily they could pull me into the circle. Subsume me. Smother me.

The memory of Casey's body, lifeless and ashen and smashed against the crib bumper, froze me in place.

Paul was close to me, and I watched with sick fascination as he tilted his head backward, face upturned to the moon. His head tilted unnaturally, then even further, contorting into a right-angle bend with his rounded shoulders. His skin rippled, the rubbery shell of his infant body stretching, straining. It quivered, a final shudder of resistance, and then cracked.

Some dark liquid—not blood, more watery than that, amniotic almost—gushed out of the wound. I recoiled, gagging. It smelled metallic and vaguely floral, like rotting lilies.

Around Paul, the others had begun to burst from their cocoons as well, the air suddenly thick with the stench. The humming grew louder. They swayed side to side, shimmying, and their skin loosened, sagged. The cracks widened to vertical gaping slits, bodies opening and drooping simultaneously.

My stomach turned. I thought I might throw up. But I couldn't stop staring, either, fixated on this transformation. This... emergence.

Paul's skin fell around him in one limp coil, like a pile of laundry, and what stood in his place was a tall, glistening dark form, its shape indescribable. It moved several limbs, shivering its segmented body. Then wings unfurled, sodden and limp at first but gaining strength as they beat against the night air.

The others emerged, following his lead. A dozen of them, hovering above the discarded husks of their infant bodies, wings beating in tandem.

I understood then where the humming had come from.

I understood, too, what they meant to do, and felt a sob catch in my throat.

"No—please. Please don't go."

Two years I had spent with them, tending them, loving them in a fashion. They had consumed my life and now, faced with their eminent departure, I imagined myself like their discarded human skins: empty, outgrown, left behind to wither and crumble.

Paul, or what had been Paul, rose in the air, wings held wide now, drying and strong. I swallowed and held my breath. Waited for him to turn to me. I don't know why I expected him to speak, or what words I expected him to say. Did I want him to thank me for sparing him? For the sacrifices I'd made, choosing his life, the lives of these other creatures, over my own well-being? That I would be spared whatever cruel fate might await the rest of humanity, because I had been so kind?

Did I expect him to tell me that he loved me? To call me "Mama" and apologize for what he'd done when he was too young to know better?

I don't know. But I got none of it.

A fledgling does not look back when it leaves the nest.

"Don't forget me," I breathed, at last, and let the tears spill over then.

They were beautiful. Unearthly and strange and living—thriving—able to fly.

The Cowbirds rose speechless into the air, assembling themselves in a flight formation. Driven by instincts unknown and incomprehensible to me. They flew up into the night, wings glinting silver-bright in the moonlight, and my heart stuttered in my chest, my belly swooping with some deep emotion.

It's only later, with tears drying on my cheeks, the outlines of the Cowbirds long since disappeared into the inky darkness, that I realized that what I was feeling was pride.

5

The Toymaker

Grandmother's house was full of wondrous toys, but Charlotte wasn't allowed to play with them.

They were kept locked up in glass cases lining every wall of the small home. They stared down at her while she slept, ate, and even when she brushed her teeth. A pair of carousel horses rode high on a shelf above the bathroom mirror, and their brown, glass-bead eyes caught the flickering light when the switch was flicked.

Charlotte asked to play with the toys once. She wanted very badly to touch a plush white bear that sat on a high shelf inside a glass case in her bedroom. The bear wore a crimson double-breasted suit vest, and his nose was covered with velvet. Charlotte thought he looked very kind, and she'd hoped he could be her friend.

But Grandmother was firm. "These are my treasures, child, not your playthings," she had said. "Run along and play with your imagination."

And so Charlotte had abandoned her hopes of befriending the soft white bear.

She did ask again, from time to time, for permission to play with some of the toys or at least to get a clearer look at them. But she always knew the answer before she even asked. Grandmother's treasures were not for playing with.

Grandmother's house was full of rules and forbidden things. Charlotte could not go into the attic, although she didn't mind that so much. It was hot and dusty up there, and it smelled like old socks; she could smell them when Grandmother opened the attic door and climbed the old ladder upstairs. Charlotte was also not to bother Grandmother in her study, although the old woman spent most of her days and nights locked up inside of it. When Charlotte stood outside the door and listened, she could sometimes hear the old woman talking to herself. The words were in another language, one she couldn't understand. Sometimes she thought she heard other people talking, their voices low whispers, but when Grandmother emerged she was always alone.

~*~

Normally, Charlotte followed the rules with no problems. But today was her birthday, and she wasn't at all pleased with the way the day had gone.

Grandmother had baked her a cake, but it was dry and crumbly. There was just one candle on it, a thick, dark, misshapen stick of wax that seemed to have been melted and reformed several times. After cake, Grandmother gave Charlotte a new dress. It was black and white, with lots of lace and a big satin bow in the back.

It was a pretty dress, in an old-fashioned sort of way—more like doll clothes than a dress for a little girl—but Charlotte wasn't satisfied with it. She was lonely. She wished that Grandmother would have given her something to play with instead.

After Charlotte put on the new dress and showed it to Grandmother, the old woman excused herself to her study and locked herself inside. Charlotte sat outside for a while, trying to wash down a slice of crumbly cake with a cup of milk, but she grew bored of it quickly. She left her cake and milk on the table and withdrew into the living room where the great oak curio cabinets were kept. She was feeling mischievous.

She stared up longingly at the glass cabinet. It was full of dolls, and they peered down at her with jewel-bright glass eyes. With their milky white skin and ornate, lacy dresses, they looked very much like Charlotte herself, and she gazed at them through her reflection in the glass.

"I wish I could play with you," she said, touching her fingertips to the wooden frame of the curio cabinet's door.

We wish we could play with you, too.

Charlotte jumped back, looking around herself in alarm. "Who's there?"

It's me, a voice said, and it was muffled as though spoken through a wall. *Llewellyn.*

"Who? I don't know anyone named Llewellyn."

Look closer. Down here—in the red dress.

Charlotte dropped to her knees to see the bottom shelf more clearly. A doll sat there, larger than the others. She wore a deep crimson dress, and a thick wave of blonde curls tumbled around her shoulders. Her cherry-red lips seemed to turn up in a slight smile, and a flicker of light caught her blue eyes as though they were alive.

See? I'm right here.

"You're a doll," Charlotte said, uncertainly. "Dolls can't talk."

Says who?

Charlotte hesitated. "You've never said anything before."

You've never listened.

Looking over her shoulder to be sure Grandmother wasn't near, Charlotte sat on the floor to be eye-level with Llewellyn. "Do all of you talk?"

Only when we have something to say.

~*~

As it turned out, Llewellyn had quite a bit to say, and Charlotte listened eagerly over the next few days as the doll filled her head with stories about all sorts of things the girl had never heard of before.

Llewellyn was very old—older even than Grandmother—and she had seen many things. She knew about exotic, faraway places and people who had fought in wars. She knew what Grandmother had been like as a little girl, and why there were so many toys in the house.

Most of the toys in this house were made by your grandmother. Did you know that? Llewellyn said. *Or by her father. They were toymakers in their village, and they made many beautiful playthings. But not me. I came to your grandmother when she was just a little girl, and I was her most precious treasure.*

Llewellyn knew a great many things about Grandmother and the way things used to be, but she rarely wanted to talk about them, no matter how much Charlotte asked. Instead, she told stories of other things she had seen, places she had been, and made promises to start answering Charlotte's more pressing questions if the girl could remove her from her glass prison. *It's easy,* Llewellyn said. *I know where the key is. Just do this for me, and I'll tell you anything you want to know.*

Charlotte was too frightened to look for the key to the curio cabinet. Instead, she would wait each day for Grandmother to shut herself away in her office, and then Charlotte would creep into the sitting room and settle down on the floor to talk with the doll. It was the closest Charlotte had ever had to a friend, and she relished these conversations, even if the doll's patience sometimes wore thin.

"If you knew my Grandmother when she was a girl," Charlotte ventured, one day when the doll seemed to be in good spirits, "Then you must have known my mother or father, too."

Llewellyn hesitated, as she often did when asked this sort of question. She tried to change the subject, but Charlotte pressed on, and finally the doll said in exasperation. *You're not ready to know about that yet.*

"What do you mean?" she asked, indignantly.

The doll fell silent for a long time, so long that Charlotte began to fear that she'd never speak again. Just as she was considering getting up to leave, Llewellyn spoke again.

I'll tell you. If you really want to know, I'll tell you. But you must do something for me first.

Charlotte didn't need to ask. She already knew: the curio cabinet key.

Llwellyn told her where to find it. The key—along with keys to every other cabinet and drawer—was in the attic. All Charlotte had to do was pull down the ladder, climb upstairs, and find the box where Grandmother had tucked it away.

It's why the attic has always been off limits to you, Llewellyn explained sensibly. *There are secrets up there, too, but I know all about them. Unlock my cabinet, and I'll tell you.*

That didn't make Charlotte feel any less frightened about the prospect, but she steeled herself. Llewellyn knew things. It was the best chance Charlotte had of ever figuring out what had happened to her parents, and she wasn't going to let a little trepidation about the attic stand in her way.

So she braced herself for the worst and went to the hall where the attic stairs pulled down from the ceiling. She had to pull a chair underneath the opening so she could tug the cord down. The stairs made so much noise that she was certain Grandmother would come, but she didn't, and once the dust settled, Charlotte was all alone.

She crept up the stairs into the attic. It was dark, lit only by a single shaft of light wafting up from the opening in the floor. The air smelled old and stale. The attic itself was small, the sloped ceiling bearing down on the room at a harsh angle. Even Charlotte had to stoop to reach the corners, and by the time she found the box Llewellyn had described, her knees were covered in dust and cobwebs.

The box rattled with the sound of keys, and she tucked it under her arm unopened. There was no point in searching for a specific key in the dark. Moving awkwardly around the cumbersome box, she made her way back toward the patch of light in the attic floor and climbed lopsidedly down. The keys rattled in the box, and Charlotte's heart began to thud with anticipation. Was Llewellyn really going to tell her about her parents?

She was so excited that she forgot to pull up the attic stairs, forgot to remove the chair she'd stepped on, forgot to dust off her cobwebby knees. She ran, rattling, into the living room, box held out so Llewellyn could see.

"I brought the box," Charlotte said. "Now, tell me about my parents."

Not so fast, Llewellyn said, and it seemed as though her painted-on smile had gone cold. *You open the door first. That's our agreement.*

"Fine," Charlotte muttered and opened the lid.

Inside were several keys, certainly, but other things were in there as well. An old-fashioned ring. A pair of glass doll eyes. Several old photographs, brown and faded with age; the corners of the paper were crumbly and yellowed.

"Who is this?" Charlotte asked uncertainly, holding up one photo. It showed a young woman with smooth, straight, dark hair and smiling creases at the corners of her eyes. She held a doll in her lap. It was very large, the size of a child, and very lifelike. The doll, like her, had straight dark hair and dark eyes, and it wore a black-and-white lacy dress with a bow. The dress looked exactly like the one she had gotten for her birthday.

With its pale skin, dark hair, and large eyes, the doll looked just like her.

Unlock the door, Llewellyn said.

Charlotte felt something swelling in her throat. It might have been fear or excitement. She couldn't tell which. She dug through the box, trying her best to ignore the photographs—each of which stared up at her with eyes that seemed all too familiar—and withdrew the key to the curio cabinet.

The lock clicked open, and it felt as though something in the house had shifted, the way a home settles when the air conditioner shuts off and the pressure releases. The old home seemed to groan with the relief of a lifted burden. Charlotte couldn't help feeling that the curio cabinet was not the only thing she had unlocked.

"There," she said, holding up two new photographs, each showing the smiling young woman and the doll that looked so very much like Charlotte. "I unlocked your door. Now tell me the truth."

You already know the truth, don't you? Llewellyn's voice rang like laughter in Charlotte's mind.

"What happened to my parents?" Charlotte's voice came out choked and hoarse.

You have no parents, Llewellyn said. *No more than I do. No more than any of the toys in this house.*

"I'm not a doll."

Are you so sure?

Frightened tears started to well up in Charlotte's eyes. But dolls didn't cry. Then again, not so long ago she had been certain that dolls didn't speak, either.

There once was a lonely toy maker, Llewellyn said. *Whose only companions were her dolls. She grew old and lonely and bitter because no one would be her friend, so she made friends for herself. She made a* child *for herself. And the child was such a wonderful toy, such a perfect replica, that eventually, the toymaker fooled even herself. Everyone forgot... Except for the oldest doll, the toy maker's first and dearest friend. She remembered and she was jealous.*

The terror gripping Charlotte then became absolute. She scrambled back from the cabinet and began to scream. She no longer cared that she was covered in dust and cobwebs, or that she would get in trouble for her foray into the attic, or even about whatever she had unleashed when she had unlocked that door.

Grandmother came, moving as swiftly as rickety old bones would allow. She looked from Charlotte sobbing on the floor, to the unlocked curio cabinet, to the scattered keys and photographs. Her brows lifted.

"Why did you do this?" she asked, and her voice was not unkind.

Tell her you were lonely.

Charlotte's mouth worked against her will. She wanted to explain about the photographs, her questions about her parents, the things the doll had told her. But what she actually said was, "I got so lonely. I just wanted something to play with."

Grandmother's expression softened. It was not a look Charlotte was accustomed to.

"Which doll were you trying to get, dear?"

Charlotte's finger trembled, but she pointed to Llewellyn, and the doll's glassy eyes shone with triumph.

We're like sisters, the doll said happily when it was clear that she wouldn't be put back into the cabinet. *Two of Grandmother's favorite toys.*

"Am I really a doll?" Charlotte whispered that night, as the two lay tucked together in bed.

Am I?

Llewellyn told many stories that night and every night after, and eventually, Charlotte stopped asking whether any of them were true.

6

Beware the Wolves

"Beware the wolves in the forest," Red's mother tells her. She fusses with her clothes, straightening her hoodie. Checking and double-checking that the supplies are packed tight in the knapsack, that there are no gaps or zippers with broken teeth. Anxiety gleams in her small, dark eyes: eyes that are hard and black like stones.

"I will," Red replies tonelessly.

Mother worries about everything. She fears the forest and its creatures. She fears the darkness and the unknown. She fears strangers and foreigners and anything else that doesn't fit inside a tiny square house with neatly-swept floors and a bright, cheery fire.

Red sneaks another glimpse at the photograph in her hands, the only one she has of her grandmother. The woman in the picture is young and handsome, with tawny hair and long, graceful limbs. She looks so much like Red it hurts. When Red looks in the mirror, she sees her grandmother's likeness, and nothing of her own mother.

It hurts Mother, she knows. Hurts her because she wanted a

baby so badly. She talks about it, sometimes, when she's caught in a wistful mood, those rare moments when she waxes nostalgic. Those times when Red catches a glimpse into her own origin story. Her mother was young, too young, too stupid and poor and naive, but she wanted the baby so badly, even though it would have been best to do away with it.

But it isn't Red's fault that unwed mothers are treated with such cruelty. It isn't her fault that she's never felt a strong bond between them. It was her mother's decision to give her life, wasn't it? Red had nothing to do with it. She feels no pressure, now, to be grateful.

~*~

She has no memory of her father. She supposes he must have looked like Grandmother, too, having been her son. There are no photographs of him anymore. Mother burned them a long time ago, said it hurt too much to think about him, to look at him. Red was barely able to rescue the snapshot of Grandmother from the pile before they all went up in flames.

In her memory, Red can barely make out an image: a large man with a grizzled mane of gray-brown hair and a thick, silvery beard. She doesn't know if the image is real or not. And sometimes, when she dreams of him, he has eyes like coins that flash golden in the dark, and a voice that growls like thunder. In her dreams, he's as big as the world, but she cannot see his face.

~*~

"Don't stray from the path. Don't talk to strangers. Don't eat anything that anyone offers you. The woods are full of tricks and liars."

"I won't," Red agrees. Her mind is elsewhere. The rules run like water through her thoughts, washing through her. Mother is always giving her rules, drawing boundaries and boxes where they don't even make sense, and Red has grown adept at ignoring them.

Her thoughts stray to the wilderness. The forest that stretches between here and there, the one where her parents met, once upon a time. When they were young and stupid in love. Or at least, that's how she chooses to think of them. It hurts too much to imagine it a different way.

~*~

"She won't look like that," Mother says, seeing her looking at the picture. "Keep that in mind. She might not be anything like what you've imagined."

"She's family," Red says, defensively. "That's all that matters to me."

"You don't have to do this," Mother says. "If you're frightened. If you're not ready."

"You said that she was dying. You said I might have no other chance to meet her."

Mother says nothing for a long time. She looks past Red, out the big window, and bites nervously at her lip. "I did. And she is. But that doesn't mean..."

She trails off, like she knows there's no point in arguing. Red has made up her mind. She has wanted so long to meet her grandmother. She has so many questions for her. Why she's been kept away from her for so long. What her father was like. Why people down in the village look at her so strangely when they ride into town. Why the other school children avoid her, whisper behind her.

"Why have you kept her from me this whole time?" Red asks, feeling bold. Knowing that her mother probably won't answer, but pressing her anyway. "Why wait until she's dying to let me have a relationship with her?"

"That road goes both ways," Mother snaps. "When your father...she could have come. Any time she wanted. She could have visited you. She could have made the effort. But she didn't, and I saw no reason to force her to."

Red is stunned by the honesty of this admission. Her mother so rarely speaks candidly.

"She wants to see you because she's dying," her mother reaffirms, and refuses to make eye contact. "There might not be much time. You'd best get on with it, if you're going."

~*~

The path is well-worn and not as dark as Red was expecting. The map guides her without incident. There are no wolves.

The sun is nearly down when Red reaches Grandmother's house. Have they always lived so close? It seems especially cruel knowing that she's had family here, all this time—just down the path, deep in the woods but plenty close enough to visit. Plenty close to have known.

The moon is visible in the darkening sky, a pale sphere that hugs close to the treeline. No smoke rises from Grandmother's chimney, no candles flicker in her windows.

Red knocks at the door.

"Come in," Grandmother's voice is a rasp.

Red hesitates. She did not expect a voice so deep and strange.

But Grandmother is ill, she reminds herself.

The house is small, all one room. The fireplace takes up one wall, with a small table and a single chair, and the bed takes up another wall, with a small dresser and a rocking chair nearby. There are no candles burning, and the only light in the room streams through the open windows, a silvery moon-glow that casts everything into deep shadow.

In the gloom, Red can hardly make out Grandmother, propped up with pillows in the bed. She seems larger than she expected. Her face is obscured in shadow.

"Who is that, now? Is that my Red?" Grandmother asks, and her voice is a low growl, as though something is caught in her throat. "Come closer, dear. I can barely see you."

"Mother said you'd be expecting me. She sent word ahead. I..." Red hesitates. What do you say to a grandmother you've never met? How do you introduce yourself to family you do not know?

"I remember you, child," Grandmother says, as if reading her thoughts. "You were too young, then, but I was there. Your father was so proud. Of all his children, you were always the most special."

"All?" Red asks, stunned. What did she mean, all?

Grandmother takes a long time to reply. She's seized by a coughing fit, long and harsh, and the bed groans in protest as her frame trembles. When she speaks, she ignores the question. Her voice is a command.

"Come on, then. Come close. Let me get a look at you and see how you've grown."

~*~

Red reluctantly eases out of her pack, setting it on the table. She takes a hesitant step forward, another, Grandmother's silhouette clearer now. She can swear she sees the triangular points of long ears at either side of her shadowy head, but that makes no sense.

"Grandmother...your ears are so large," she says, surprising herself; she had not meant to say this.

"So are yours, my dear," Grandmother rasps.

Red touches a hand to her ear, half certain that she will feel the velvet of fur against her fingertips—but she does not. They are the same ears she has always had, round and smooth and tucked away beneath her hoodie.

She crosses the room. The moon is higher in the sky, now, at a better angle to shine through the window, and the silvery gleam catches upon Grandmother's eyes, which glow green-gold from the shadows of her face. "Grandmother!" Red says, "Your eyes are so bright!"

"So are yours."

Grandmother shifts upon her pillows, turning her yellow-green eyes onto her granddaughter. She smiles, and the opalescent glow of the moon reflects upon her teeth. They are long and sharp.

"Your teeth are so sharp..." Red says. She realizes that she is standing at the bedside, and the creature in the bed looks nothing like any grandmother she could have imagined. It does not even look human. It has long, triangular ears and a broad snout and a gaping maw filled with silver-white teeth. It has silky gold-brown fur and bright yellow-green eyes with pupils like slits.

"As are yours, my dear," Grandmother says, enveloping Red's hand in her own. The fingers are stubby and end in dull black claws.

"You're not human," Red says, feeling the claws curl around her arm, feeling surprising strength in the creature's grasp. "You're not my grandmother. You can't be."

"I'm as human as you are," she says. Her claws tighten. "As human as your father."

That gets her attention. Red swallows hard, staring down at the monster in the bed.

Something like a smile curls up the sides of Grandmother's toothy maw. "You have the wolf in you. I knew you would. Your father—he was sure you wouldn't. Demanded I stay away from you, no matter what, so you could live a normal life. So you could be just like your mother. Just like the human he fell in love with. But that's not what you want, is it? There's a wildness in you. I can smell it."

The speech takes a lot out of her. She's breathless when it finishes. She sucks in a deep, rattling gasp. Air whistles through her long snout.

Red stares at her, shocked. Uncomprehending. Her head swims with questions, so many. Too many to ask. She settles for the simplest.

"What did you mean, 'all?' Is there...do I have more family?"

"Oh, child." Grandmother pulls her closer. "Your mother was not his first, or his only. But she was special to him. He'd want you to know that."

She thinks of the wolf song outside her window at night, the voices raised against the wind on nights her mother warned her not to go outside. A part of her always thought there was something familiar in their cry. A part of her always thought they were howling just for her.

"I have so many questions," Red says. She should be frightened of the thing in the bed. It should repulse her. But she has a sudden longing to lean close, to bury her head in her fur, to cuddle against her warmth and breathe deep.

~*~

She spends the night talking with her grandmother. It goes slowly, broken by coughing fits, but they get through years of missing time. They rest often so Grandmother can close her eyes, slip away to sleep, and every time Red worries she won't wake up. Worries she'll pass away before she can answer all of her questions.

But it's a foolish worry. It would be impossible to answer all of her questions, no matter how much time they have.

But piece by piece, answer by answer, the details begin to fill in. They are as wondrous as they are mundane. Once upon a time, a wolf who walked like a man met a woman in the forest. Once upon a time, they fell in love, and he thought he could live among her kind, thought he could choose a different kind of life if he started the right kind of family.

He was wrong, and selfish, to take that kind of risk. Both of them were. But there had been real love, whatever monstrous stories the village came up with. And when the woodsmen tracked him down, slaughtering him like an animal for the sin of living among men, his wife wept in secret, too frightened of their judgment to tell them they'd done wrong.

~*~

"There isn't much time left," Grandmother says, sparing a glance toward the window. It's darkening again.

Have they spent a whole day together, already? Time grows slippery when it's stretched between memories. Red has drowsed often today, following her grandmother's rhythm, but she's certain that she's awake now. She has never felt so alert. So alive. Her nerves sing with anticipation.

"You know enough now," Grandmother continues. "Enough to decide. If you want…If you want to go home now, to live among men, you are free. But if you want…another life…you have to choose. Quickly. While there's still time."

Red thinks of the darkness between the trees. She thinks of her dreams, the monstrous shape with golden eyes, huge but friendly and familiar. She thinks of the smell of summer grass and the call of wolves and the way she has never felt quite right in her skin.

"It won't hurt, will it?"

"Only for a moment."

She thinks of her mother, the way she couldn't even meet her eyes when she departed. Thinks of her bitter disappointment: this child she risked everything for, who could not even love her the way she wanted. She tries to imagine her mother's grief, knowing she will never come home.

But her mother's feelings are no longer her burden to bear. They never should have been.

"Do it," Red whispers.

Her heart thuds beneath her ribs. Her pulse rushes in her ears like an incoming tide.

Grandmother's claws curl into her skin. She draws Red close, her maw open wide. Her breath is warm and damp. Her sharp teeth cut into Red's skin.

It doesn't hurt.

Or, rather, it does—but it is magnificent, a consuming tearing pain, the agony of birth.

Grandmother tears away the skin and Red emerges from within herself, as whole and complete as a little bird birthed from an egg. Her senses sharpen. Her bones lengthen and shift, allowed at last to unfurl from the tight cage they've been trapped within. She drops to all fours and shakes herself, feeling the ripple of life like electricity shifting through her golden fur.

She has long, pointed ears and sharp, white teeth and her eyes gleam like silver dollars in the dark.

As the moon rises over the cabin, the wolf song begins in the forest, a cacophony of voices. Red's brothers and sisters, aunts and uncles. A whole family she'd never been allowed to know. One whose absence she had always felt, deep down, in the wolf parts that lurked under her skin.

Grandmother joins in, her voice feeble. She calls out to the others, letting them know that Red has come home. She doesn't have much life left in her, but Red will spend the remaining hours at her side. Then she will step outside, the earth beneath her paws, and find a new place in this world.

She lifts her muzzle and adds her voice to the chorus.

7

The Twins

As deep as it was in the woods, it took a long time for anyone to find the body. The old widow woman—there had been rumors she was a witch, and rumors still that she had gotten her due—had lived alone for a long, long time, and few people in the forest knew her. Fewer still could be bothered to care, even when the news broke that her twisted, charred remains had been pulled from her own oven in the burnt-out husk of what had once been her house.

And so, no one thought to look too deeply into what had happened. Certainly no one noticed the footprints leading away, small and lock-step like two children moving arm-in-arm through the loam of the forest.

The children, for their part, gave little heed to what others might think. It was not their way. For so long as they had ever lived, they'd had each other, and that was all they needed. The sharpness of their teeth, glittering needles that flashed in darkness, punctuated their self-sufficiency.

They walked a long time from the woods, away from the smoke curling from the witch's house, the barbecue-sweet smell of cooking flesh. They followed lesser-known trails, walking through the night and into the light of day where the path grew broader and the trees grew further apart and grass sprouted in the sunny places.

There was another house there, the honest cabin of a working man and his wife, and the twins gave each other sidelong glances and approached it in silence, for they had learned that adults preferred children to be seen and not heard.

Besides. It was so much easier this way.

The man found them first, two children alone in the woods, and after some hesitation he relented, because what kind of monster would leave them alone against the elements and wild animals, whoever they were?

His wife fussed over them, as he expected her to, and they brought them into the home, a part of the family, however much it strained their finances to keep them fed.

And they were so very, very hungry.

"I don't know if we can afford to keep feeding them," the wife said, in a hushed voice, hopeful that the sleeping children would not hear. "They eat so much."

But the children never slept, and they always listened.

It was how they had survived so long.

In the day, everyone smiled, pretending that things were fine. A happy family, normal and secure.

The twins would bide their time. They could be very patient, when they wanted to be.

In time, no one would ever think to notice or connect the fires in the woods, the bodies burned to a crisp, or the bites of flesh missing from their remains.

8

Camp Tailypo

"Come on! Pick up your feet!" Coach Mackey yells. "Do you call that running? What are you going to do if your life depends on it? Lay down and die?"

Is that a threat? I can only half-wonder, because I'm struggling just to keep up with the instructions he's yelling in-between his weirdly ominous pep-talk. My chest feels like it's about to burst and my legs are burning, but the last person around the track has to run an extra lap as punishment so I'm pushing myself hard.

"Do you think your ancestors lived and died for you to fatten up on Cheetos in front of the TV? No! They would be ashamed to see how you all turned out! None of you would last five minutes living off the land! The only thing keeping you alive right now is other people's hard work."

Coach Mackey is big and broad and muscular, with veins popping out in his neck and arms that barely squeeze into his tracksuit. He's a retired bodybuilder, a fitness coach, and apparently also an armchair anthropologist. I still think "fitness coach" is a stupid term, because how can you be a coach without a team or even a sport? But then I guess "fitness" is a sport in the same way that Camp Tallyho is a summer camp, which is not really at all.

If you hadn't seen the brochure calling this place a "teen fitness retreat"—and you overlooked the part where everybody here is fat—you could probably mistake Camp Tallyho for a regular summer camp. It's out in the woods, a campground tucked away at the end of a dusty road, with a big wooden sign at the entrance. The sign should read "Camp Tallyho," but somebody vandalized it, scratching deep in the wood to make it look like "Camp Tailypo" instead, whatever that's supposed to mean.

But Camp Tallyho is a fitness boot camp. A summer-long program where parents send their fat kids, hoping to get skinny kids returned back to them. Like one of those wilderness survival camps they send troubled teens to as punishment, except our only crime is having bigger bodies than they think we should.

Coach Mackey's whistle blows. "That's enough. Hit the showers. Now I can see I've got my work cut out for me. Tomorrow, the real fun begins."

I can't imagine what kind of sadistic plan constitutes "fun" in his mind. But I'm relieved to be done with today. I stumble off the path cut through pine trees and double over, trying to catch my breath. Emma flops down on the forest floor, wheezing with effort. She's getting pine needles all in her hair, but I don't think she cares.

"I never want to run again in my entire life," she pants. "Something comes after me...and I'm just...gonna...die."

She lets her tongue loll out dramatically. I know exactly what she means.

~*~

Emma is one of my bunk mates. The other one is Alice, who's a couple years younger than me, short and plump and nervous like a little dormouse. She's been velcroed to my side pretty much since I got here, and she's terminally cringe, but I can't help feeling a little protective of her.

We've got an assigned counselor, too. Every cabin has one. Most of the counselors here are kind of creepy, all Stepford smiles and enthusiasm, but Cassie's all right. She's got curly hair and tawny skin and the kind of big, thick legs you get from playing a lot of soccer. She's only a couple years older than us, I think.

I expected her to hassle us every night with pep-talks or shame us about our weekly weigh-ins, but mostly she just hangs out in her bunk and reads paperbacks and leaves us alone. She even looks the other way when Emma hauls out her shoebox of contraband snacks—her dad sends care packages to sneak in candy bars and donuts, because he didn't approve of his ex-wife sending her to fat camp. Emma told us the whole story while handing out rolls of mini powdered donuts, the gas station kind.

"How did you come to work here, anyway?" I asked Cassie, after she introduced herself that first day. "I mean. No offense. But aren't you like, almost our same age?"

"It's my first year doing this, yeah. I used to be a camper. I kept showing up every summer and they gave me a job." She grinned. "This is actually the first time they've gone all-in with this camping thing. Normally it's down at the college, staying in dorms and using the gym and stuff. But I guess they got a really good deal buying this place, and thought it'd get more people to sign up. I dig it. It's...rustic."

"So why was it so cheap? Is it haunted or something? Is some dude with a chainsaw going to rise up from the lake and murder us all?"

Cassie frowned, her brows knitting. "You know, actually, there is this one thing…I don't know if this is really why. But back before, when Camp Tallyho was just a regular summer camp, some kids did die here. They drowned in the lake, I guess. They went out for a swim late at night and never came back. They never found their bodies, either. Just put up all those no-swimming signs."

Emma perked up. "So their rotting corpses are probably still down there. Oooooh!"

Alice squeaked. Emma stuck her tongue out.

"That is so not funny."

"True story, though." Cassie nodded, looking suddenly solemn. "So definitely stay away from the lake."

~*~

After dinner, the counselors lead us all in a big group to the fire pit set up out past the lake. Well, "lake" is just what everybody calls it. It's actually more of a big, mossy pond with a bunch of weeds growing around it. There are "no swimming" signs posted everywhere, but I can't imagine anyone actually wanting to. It looks like the kind of place you'd pick up leeches or a brain-eating amoeba.

Or a place where you could drown and leave your rotting skeleton behind forever, apparently.

Why didn't they dredge the lake, I wonder? If some kids really did die down there, why not go pull up the bodies? I heard once about a lake in Colorado where a ton of toxic waste got dumped from a factory or something. The whole thing is practically radioactive. So they can't drag the lake without poisoning people. If you drown, your body just has to sink down to the bottom with all the other radioactive sludge or whatever.

Maybe that's the deal here, too. Maybe the lake is radioactive.

Or maybe Emma and Cassie were just fucking with me about the drowned kids. I'll have to look it up when they let me out of here and I get my iPhone back.

Luckily the smell of wood smoke is enough to drown out the fishy pond stench coming up off the water, and the air is warm and cozy. The whole forest around us pretty much disappears into darkness once the sun goes down, so the world is confined just to what's inside the fire's nice orange glow. Something could be out there, I think, in the darkness, watching us all assemble here, and we'd never even know.

~*~

The bonfire is our weekly celebration, they tell us. It's our weigh-in day treat. When we showed up, everybody had to get weighed and measured like cattle at a livestock show. Then every Friday, they repeat this indignity, marking down our "progress" on a chart. So they can encourage us, supposedly. Or so they can send reports back to our parents, make sure they feel they're getting their money's worth.

I claim a seat near the fire on one of the benches carved out of a log. The seat isn't quite wide enough, so I have to keep squirming and shifting my weight to keep my butt-cheeks from going numb, but it's better than sitting on the ground.

Alice and Emma find me and take seats nearby. Emma has a pack of marshmallows and a fist full of sticks, and I figure it's more contraband before I realize that other people have them, too. I guess even fat camp lets you roast marshmallows on weigh-in day. How generous of them.

Cassie catches up with us.

"Well, girls, how's your first week of camp been treating you?"

"Like dogshit," Emma replies cheerfully. She sticks her marshmallow straight in the fire, lighting it like a torch, and watches as the outside blackens and blisters before blowing it out.

Some counselors are trying to get campers to sing. Coach Mackey has a guitar laid over his lap and he's strumming it with the confidence of a guy who everybody's too afraid to be honest with. He strikes up a random chord and starts crooning "The Ants Go Marching" like we're a bunch of five-year-olds. I scoot as far away from that as possible.

"We should tell ghost stories," Emma suggests, loading up a fresh marshmallow. "It would be a waste of a perfectly good bonfire not to tell one."

"I don't know any stories," I say.

"Tell one that isn't super scary!" Alice whines.

"Let's see..well, we're out in the woods...so that calls for cryptids," Emma decides, matter-of-factly. She starts listing things off on her fingers. "Bigfoot. Mothman. Ogopogo. Tailypo."

"Wait, what was that last one?"

"Tailypo?"

"Yeah," I say. "I saw that here. Where it says Camp Tallyho. Somebody scratched it out to say Tailypo instead. What the heck does that even mean?"

"It's just some weird local legend," Cassie says.

"What?" Emma asks, sounding genuinely shocked. "You

don't know about the tailypo?"

"No...?"

"It's this, like. Really old story. About this old hermit who lives by himself up in the mountains with just three big hunting dogs for company. One day he's out hunting and sees some big animal and shoots at it, but misses and just manages to shoot off its tail."

"I don't know how that even works but okay, sure."

"Anyway," she shoots me a silencing look, then adjusts her posture, totally getting into storytelling mode. "He figures, hey, this is a big meaty tail, might as well cook it up for supper. So he tosses it into the stew pot that night and eats it up, and feeds the bones to his dogs."

"Ew."

She ignores me. "So that night, he wakes up and sees this big hulking animal in his room. All he can really make out is its silhouette and its eyes, which glow in the dark like embers. Probably some kind of demon. But it can talk, like sort of in a growl, 'My tailypo, my tailypo, give me back my tailypo.' And the hunter's like, screw this, and sics one of his dogs on it. The dog manages to chase the thing outside and they fight, but the dog doesn't come back. The monster just keeps coming. He does this twice, and the third time the dog doesn't even listen to his command. It just runs off, terrified, leaving him all alone."

"How did the dogs get outside? Can they work doorknobs, or..."

"Shush. Anyway, so the man and the monster are alone together now in the dark, and the monster's like, 'Tailypo, my tailypo, give me back my tailypo' and the hunter is like, 'I don't have it, I ate it, I can't give it to you.' So the monster gobbles him up."

"That's it?"

Emma shrugs. "Sometimes it tears him open and eats his guts out, to get its tail back. Sometimes it destroys the whole cabin with its attack somehow, so that the only thing anybody ever finds is rubble."

"What a stupid story. What's even the point of that?"

"A warning not to take things that don't belong to you, I guess," Cassie says.

"Or not to eat whatever weird shit you find lying around," Emma says. "The same as that one about the big toe. Or the one where the guy takes a liver off a corpse at the gallows. Even back when people were starving half the time, folks still thought up ways to guilt-trip them about what they were eating."

I notice that Alice looks a few shades paler than normal. "You know a lot of creepy stories, huh."

"I guess," Emma admits. "Why? Do you want to hear another one?"

Alice interrupts. "N-no thank you. If it's all right, I think...can we talk about something else now?"

"Fine by me." Emma gets up from her seat on the bench and stretches. Her shirt rides up over her belly, and she tugs it back down, absently. "In fact, I was just heading over to go see what the guys are up to over there. Maybe I can convince them to come play truth-or-dare." She winks. "Anybody else wanna come?"

Cassie rolls her eyes and stands to follow her. "I guess I'd better go and supervise that."

They vanish into a cluster of boys on the far side of the fire, and I go back to my marshmallow. Beside me, Alice has drawn her arms up into her sleeves, like she's suddenly chilled, and I ask if she'd like to just go back to the cabin. She looks like she was waiting her whole life for me to ask, and we blow off the rest of the bonfire before someone has a chance to coerce me into singing "Kumbaya."

~*~

Late in the night, I'm woken by the sound of screams.

I sit bolt upright, smacking my head on the bunk overhead. I fall back onto my pillow, grimacing as I hold a hand to the stinging lump on my forehead, and try to make sense of the noise.

It's Alice. Screeching like a banshee and thrashing around in the overhead bunk. The mattress squeaks with every movement.

"The tailypo! The tailypo!" she yells.

"Oh for god's sake…"

I roll sideways out of my bunk, still grimacing at the throbbing pain in my head. Alice is thrashing around in the top bunk, whimpering and crying out, eyes screwed shut, clearly caught in the grip of a nightmare. I reach out to grab her shoulder and shake it, hard, before she has a chance to thrash her way out of bed and fall.

"Alice, wake up. You're having a bad dream."

She jerks, eyes flying open, and stares uncomprehendingly at me, slack-jawed and blinking. The confusion clears slowly, replaced with embarrassment.

"I saw…" she starts, then trails off, looking away.

"Just a dream," I say, but follow her gaze, and frown. All that racket should have woken the others, but there's no sign of movement coming from that side of the room—because the beds are empty. Emma and Cassie are gone.

Alice slithers out of her bunk, landing with a thud as her socked feet hit the floor. She swipes an arm over her eyes and makes a quiet little whimper noise.

"They probably just had to pee," I say, trying to hide the uncertainty in my voice. Hoping she won't notice that the beds are still made, like nobody ever slept in them. Like Emma and Cassie never came back from the bonfire. "Put on your shoes. We'll go find them."

I grab a flashlight from my backpack and flick it on, checking the batteries. Double-check that the beds are empty. Yes and yes.

Alice clinging in close beside me, I creep outside and start toward the outhouses. No signs of life. No movement. We creep out further, headed toward the fire pit. There's no smoke and no orange light; the fire's been out for a while. We're close to the lake now, near the path that curves around it, connecting the two sides of the campground.

Something moves in the trees. My skin goes cold.

I wheel around to look, heart leaping into my throat.

The flashlight beam bounces over two lumpy silhouettes, frozen in place like scared rabbits. Cassie and Emma, fully dressed, stare at the two of us in our pajamas and wild bed hair.

"What are you doing out here?" I glance up at the sky, where the moon is high and bright, and point to it. "Where have you been?"

I have no idea what time it is, how long I've been asleep, but it seems late. Relief is flooding through me, but I'm pissed, too, because how dare they make me be the mom-friend? And also how dare they scare me half to death in the dark?

"We snuck over to the boy's side," Emma admits. "We've been playing spin-the-flashlight."

"She was sneaking," Cassie clarifies. "I was trying to stop

her."

"You're kind of a terrible counselor, did you know that?"

"Shh! Did you hear that?" Alice asks.

I wave at them to hush, straining to listen. Alice is right. I definitely picked up a sound nearby. Voices, hard to make out through the wind in the trees, but distinct. And a faint stench of something burning—like cigarette smoke, but stronger, skunkier.

"Is somebody smoking a joint?" Emma asks, sounding jealous.

"Over there!" I point.

There's a couple counselors strolling nearby. I grab Alice and drag her back into the underbrush so they don't see us, but they don't look too concerned with finding out-of-bounds campers. They're hand-in-hand, and the girl keeps leaning on the guy's arm and whispering into his ear, then bursting into giggles. They stop under a big tree, him pushing her back against the broad trunk and her not resisting in the slightest, yielding under his touch.

"I don't think they're gonna notice us," I mutter. I start to turn to climb back out onto the path, ready to head back to bed.

But then Cassie shushes me and jabs an elbow hard into my side, pointing at the lake.

The scummy surface quivers in the moonlight, the mossy algae swelling like a big bubble. But it's not a bubble, it's something living. Something huge.

It moves to the water's edge and climbs onto the bank, a big hulking dark shape dripping with tangled weeds. It's the size of a bear, but shaped more like a gorilla; its back slopes and its forelimbs are longer than the hind legs. Each beefy arm ends in a sharp, bird-like grasping talon. The thing lumbers forward, a heavy head with a pig-like snout and huge, curving tusks.

It moves fast, faster than anything that big has any right to move.

The counselors don't have time to see it coming. It charges them. I can see a flash of white in the girl's eyes, reflecting the moonlight. Wide and scared looking over the guy's shoulder, but before she can make a sound the creature has slammed face-first into them, its long goring tusk slicing neatly through the guy's body, pinning the two of them together, tangling their guts. The creature tosses its head, dislodging the counselors, and begins to paw and tear at them with its sharp talons, a big long tail swishing back and forth behind like an agitated cat's.

"It's the tailypo," Alice whimpers, and then she can't hold in the horror anymore. She screams before I can get my hand over her mouth, and the creature lifts its head and swings its gaze around curiously to look for us. Its nostrils flare. It snuffles, then paws at the earth, like an angry bull getting ready to charge.

"Shiiiiiiiit," Emma breathes.

Cassie grabs her and me both by the collar and jerks us back. "Run!"

I barely think to grab Alice's hand, yanking her along with us, as the four of us crash and stumble through the undergrowth. Twice, Emma trips, ripping open the knee of her jeans on some bushes, skinning the palm of her hand. She leaves a bright smear of blood behind as she scrambles back to her feet.

The monster is right behind us, and the only thing giving us an advantage is the brush. We duck and dodge through it as best we can, but the tailypo just plows straight through. That slows it down, but not by nearly enough.

We hit open ground, the last stretch between the woods and our cabin, and even though my legs are screaming at me to stop and my heart is hammering so hard in my chest I think I'm going to die, I give it everything I've got to clear that distance.

It's not enough. I'm not going to make it—

"You there!" A light bobs and flashes over us. Coach Mackey is standing up ahead, wearing a gray tracksuit and a stern expression. "What are you girls doing out at night?"

Before any of us can even think of answering, his gaze slides off of us and onto the thing behind us, and his jaw drops.

"Run!" he yells, as if it wasn't obvious what we were already doing. I don't dare look back, but I can hear the creature change course, hear the heavy fall of its steps as it shifts its focus onto this loud distraction. I feel the warmth radiating off its slimy, pond-scummy body as it barrels toward him, and take that opportunity to close the distance to the cabin.

Alice is limping, clutching at a stitch in her side. I grab her arm and tug her along, shoving her ahead of me. I dare to cast one glance back at Coach Mackey.

I see him roll up his sleeves, ball up his fists. He drops down into boxer's stance, ready to throw hands with the monster. His muscles bulge beneath the track suit, and under a thin shaft of moonlight it looks like he's prepared his whole life for this moment, this fight of a lifetime.

It's over within seconds.

The creature plows through him without slowing. There's an awful, wet shredding sound, punctuated by gurgling, choked-off screams. I can smell it even from here—that metallic tang of blood, the acrid stench of guts being torn open. Like an outhouse turned over. Like rotten meat left in the sun.

I turn away and try not to puke.

The screaming ceases. There's another sound that follows it. Crunching. Grinding. Chewing.

We get to the cabin door and Cassie paws at it with numb, trembling fingers a couple of times before she manages to work the knob. We tumble into it, one at a time, and as I cross the threshold I dare to cast a glance back over my shoulder, seeking the creature in the darkness.

The ground around it is lumpy and stained dark, the blood black under the moonlight. Its face and chest are covered in it. It snorts, shaking its shaggy body like a wet dog. It paws at the ground, the glowing embers of its eyes locked on us.

It charges.

We get the door slammed shut just in time for the creature to smash into it. It rattles on its hinges. Wood cracks and splinters. Sharp talons scrape against the rough wood, the tips slicing through like butter.

"It's gonna be through that door in like two seconds," Cassie says. "Look for a weapon! Something!"

Alice is a quivering, useless mess next to me, and it's taking everything I have just to keep breathing. It feels like my ribs are getting crushed, like my lungs are being wrung out to dry, and all I can think of is what that monster's tusks looked like slicing through two human bodies like they were nothing.

The door splinters, and the tailypo thrusts its broad, shaggy face inside. Its nostrils flare. It shakes its head from side to side, snorting and pawing. It'll be through the door frame any second now, and then it's going to rip through all four of us like the rotator blade on a fancy blender.

Emma chucks her shoebox of snacks at the creature's head.

It jerks, startled by the sound of the cardboard thumping against the floor. Its nostrils flare. It huffs, then snuffles its pig snout over the contents, temporarily distracted.

"That's it. Now go, go, go," Cassie urges. She works open the back window and starts heaving herself up over the frame. Her feet scramble for purchase, and I surge forward to give them a shove, helping her tumble out onto the ground outside. I follow after, my body twisting and squeezing and contorting with the effort, and I know I'm going to be bruised in a million places but at least nothing's broken. Emma practically lobs Alice outside, and then we all three reach in to grab her and haul her out.

We collapse, panting, onto the forest floor. I'm covered in sap and pine needles and mud and my legs are quivering.

"The other kids," Alice says. "They don't...they don't know. We have to..."

We have to do something. It's what she can't bring herself to say, but she's right. But what can we do? What can four chubby teenagers do against a giant bladed beast of death?

The sound of rustling plastic and low grunts of pleasure make it clear what's happening inside. The tailypo is making short work of the snack stash.

"I think it's hungry," I say, trying to focus on what it's doing now and not on the image of blood spraying everywhere from it ripping through those poor counselors. What it did to Coach Mackey. What it's going to do to us. "Like...hungry in a really, really angry way."

"I can sympathize," Emma quips.

But Cassie's got a thoughtful look. "There's a ton of food at the mess hall. If we can lure it over there, and get the door unlocked somehow, maybe we can trap it...?"

Trap it, and then do what?

And what if we can't get the door open in time?

Alice had called it the tailypo, and I know it's just because of that stupid story, but what if she was right? That thing came up out of the lake. What if those campers didn't drown? What if they got eaten? What if "Camp Tailypo" wasn't vandalism, but was some kind of warning?

Think. Think!

In the story, that monster attacked the guy with so much force that it destroyed his entire cabin. He couldn't fight it off even with his hunting dogs.

Then again...the dogs went in one by one. What if they'd all attacked at once?

What if the point of the story isn't about eating the wrong thing at all, but a warning against trying to survive all by yourself? If that guy hadn't been a mountain hermit, maybe he wouldn't need to eat some weird monster's tail just to get by.

"Wait, that's it." I climb up to my feet, heart and mind both racing. "The thing came up out of the water and rushed at those counselors, then came charging after us. It changed course from us to Coach Mackey. It ignored us to eat the snacks. It seems like it has a really short attention span. Any one of us up against this thing would be toast. But it can't attack all of us."

I explain the plan as quick as I can. I hope they get what I mean. The tailypo has gone through everything in the snack box and has started backpedaling, trying to squeeze its big body back out of the splintered door. We come in pairs around each side of the cabin.

"Hey!" I yell, and the beast lifts its shaggy head and turns toward me, starting to lumber close.

"Over here, asshole!" Emma yells, from the opposite direction.

The tailypo whirls around to look at her.

I take a step back. Alice breaks away from me, trembling, and yells. Cassie echoes from across the way.

The tailypo, confused, whirls around in a circle, its gaze

darting between the four of us. It can't decide which one of us to chase.

Other campers start coming out of their cabins, sleepy and confused and scared. But they see what we're doing, and it doesn't take too long for them to start to figure it out. Somebody hurls a rock at the creature, and then everyone is grabbing rocks and sticks and shoes and anything else they can find.

I think of a cave painting I saw once in school, showing how the cavemen killed the giant mastodon. How a whole band of hunters worked together to drive the creature over a cliff, or surround it and stab it with spears until it fell to its knees. No one person could kill a mastodon. But together, a tribe could bring one down.

~*~

Twenty fat kids descend on a monster, and together we drive it back into the dark.

Disoriented, confused by the loud, angry crowd and with its sides stinging from the barrage of projectiles, the tailypo retreats from camp. It slinks, limping, back to the lake, and we give chase, moving slow but sure through the crushed undergrowth until we're certain the thing has gone so far underwater that it's out of reach.

We make it back to camp in one piece, tired and aching but alive. Someone finds the emergency phone in the main hall and calls for help, and soon enough the place is swarming with park rangers, cops, animal control, ambulances. Then parents, panicked and confused and exhausted from being pulled from their beds.

Officially, the story is that a bear got into camp and mauled two counselors and a fitness coach to death. Officially, it's a tragic accident. The camp will be shut down, the parents refunded, and a bunch of kids will go back to their separate lives and maybe some will forget what really happened tonight.

But I won't, and neither will Alice and Emma and Cassie.

Because Coach Mackey was dead wrong about our ancestors. About survival. In the end, surviving Camp Tailypo wasn't about being strong, or fast, or making some big heroic last stand. We made it because a bunch of fat kids stuck together. And whatever stories they tell, whatever lies they try to make us believe about what happened here, that's what I'm gonna remember.

9

Not Even Once

"Stay away from psychedelics," Mr. Murphy, the health class teacher, was always fond of saying. "Because as soon as you try them, there's no going back. Your brain will never be the same after even just one drop of acid."

Then he'd tell us some horrifying story about an acid-tripping babysitter who put a spiral ham in the high chair and the baby in the oven. Or some guy in a psychiatric hospital, convinced he was a glass of orange juice—unable to lay flat because he was afraid he'd spill out.

We'd laugh at the stories, because they were ridiculous, and he'd scowl like he was deadly serious.

"I've seen some things you wouldn't believe," Mr. Murphy would always say, and then just shake his head and get back to his lecture. It was just about the only part of his lessons that ever stuck with me. With health class in fourth period, right after lunch, my brain was always checked out. Sometimes I'd walk out afterward pretty sure I'd fallen asleep for half the class because, honestly? I couldn't tell you a single thing we ever learned about in health class other than drugs.

~*~

Taking peyote at lunch hadn't really been my plan for the day. I'd never tried it, and hallucinogens weren't normally my thing. But getting hold of anything was hard these days after Kyle got busted selling dollar joints in the parking lot. Mr. Murphy had caught him, of course, and everyone knew what a hard-ass he was. Kyle got suspended so hard his parents must have moved school districts because we never heard from him after.

The D.A.R.E. guys started coming around campus more after that, doing locker and bag checks, and Mr. Murphy really doubled down on his "drugs are bad" speeches, and nobody else so much as toked under a bleacher for a long time until Aaron moved in from out of town and brought his exotic shit with him.

Aaron's parents were total hippies who didn't care what he did. He had blue hair and did his eyeliner in permanent marker because, according to him, you get a contact high through your mucus membranes. He had a lot of friends, the kind of friends who could get him all sorts of stuff.

Like the bag of peyote currently in my hand.

"This is some powerful shit," Aaron warned when he sold it to me. "It'll open up your mind. Make you see shit in the fifth dimension. Total spiritual experience. Transcendent. You'll never see the world the same again after."

Anyway. I should have waited until I got home. But I was bored and curious, and figured anything that could make Mr. Murphy's class more interesting was worth trying. It kind of felt like giving him the finger, doing this thing he hated so much, and that thrill was half the fun.

~*~

I put the first peyote button in my mouth and chewed. It was dry and rubbery and tasted disgusting but I swallowed it down, then the second one.

I waited. I stared at the mirror. I thought about how when you do Bloody Mary you see a face pop up behind you. I freaked out and whirled around to look. Just double-checking, but of course nobody was there. I was being paranoid.

Was paranoia a side effect of doing peyote? Did that mean it was working?

I wheeled back around. Stared at myself again.

Felt the world start to shift around me, like going sideways. Felt a pressure build up in my ears, or my jaw, or my throat. Somewhere. Like my mouth watering. And then my stomach heaved and I whirled around and smashed my face into the toilet stall door and fell hard to my knees just in time to blow chunks.

Aaron had forgotten to warn me about that part, that asshole.

~*~

I made it to class just after the bell rang. Clammy, watery-eyed, sure to be busted. But Mr. Murphy didn't say anything as I took my seat. He barely looked my way at all. A uniformed shadow moved in the hall. Four sets of toenails clattered on the linoleum outside the door.

The D.A.R.E. guy and his dog in for a surprise bag check. Of course.

The room had the usual after-lunch energy slump, like everybody there wanted to be somewhere else, or was mentally already checked out. The chatter of my classmates was a discordant hum that hushed down to silence as the uniformed officer walked in.

Around me, my classmates fell eerily silent, staring ahead in unison, vacant-eyed, slack-jawed. Like somebody had hit pause on the room. The cop started down the row, stopping at the first desk, and the kid didn't flinch. Didn't acknowledge him at all, actually, just stared straight ahead. The cop's boots thumped the linoleum, the dog's claws tapping, its harness jingling. Otherwise, the room had gone completely, deafeningly silent.

Thump, thump. Jingle, jingle.

I looked down at the dog and felt my insides seize up and flip over and for a minute I thought I was going to throw up again.

At a glance, the dog seemed fine. A perfectly normal German Shepherd. But the longer I looked at him, the more seemed to be wrong. The general impression was right, but the details were all jumbled. His body stretched, thin and drooping like taffy, and he seemed to have a varying number of limbs, sometimes three, sometimes five. His outline flickered, like he was right on the verge of turning into something else, or like he was cloaked by some disguise that mapped poorly onto his body.

The dog stopped, tilted its head up toward me. It had no eyes, and its face split vertically, a long wet tongue lolling from the pink gash where its mouth should be.

I wanted to scream, but I couldn't make a sound. I couldn't turn my head, but my eyes darted around, panicked. I flicked my gaze up to the clock, saw the second hand take its slow time ticking forward, like it was struggling against a terrible weight holding it in place.

It's the peyote. It's the peyote, I chanted in my head, gripping the desk with both white-knuckled hands.

The dog paused at each desk, carefully touching its ruined, heaving nostrils to the backpacks, shoes, pants legs. The D.A.R.E cop, his face a shadow that would not reconcile into features, followed solemnly behind, touching each kid's head with an impossibly broad hand, elongated fingers bending at improbable joints.

The students, hair tousled, continued staring ahead blankly, as if caught in amber. Like time stopped moving when the dog entered the room. Something silvery flowed up and around the cop's forearm, like a pale slug crawling up out of each kid's head and writhing up the cop's wrist. He tilted his head back as if in ecstasy each time, then made his way to the next desk.

Is this why I could never seem to remember anything that happened in this class? Had this happened before, and last time I'd been one of those slack-jawed, empty-eyed classmates?

"Hey," the cop said, coming up even with my desk. "There's something wrong with this one."

The dog touched its nose to my pants leg. The cop grabbed my chin in his hand, pulled down a lower eyelid with one spindly thumb. I tried not to stare into the gaping black void where his face should be, but it was impossible to look away while he examined me.

Sweat prickled my forehead. My heart thumped so hard I thought it would explode. I couldn't move. Could barely breathe.

Mr. Murphy made an impatient noise. "Not again. I swear, it's getting harder and harder to get kids who haven't taken anything."

"Once they see through us, they're useless," the cop sulked.

"Nobody would believe him," Mr. Murphy said, hopeful. "We could just write it off as a bad trip?"

"His brains are still ruined. They'll never taste the same. And what if he sees the principal? We can't risk that before the graduation harvest."

Mr. Murphy sighed in defeat. "I know, I know. Fine. Let's get it over with, then. I'll arrange to deal with the parents tonight."

The faceless D.A.R.E. officer's huge hand enveloped the back of my neck, fingers digging in. He dragged me from my desk and pushed me down to my knees, forcing me to kneel before Mr. Murphy's approaching form.

Mr. Murphy paused in front of me, loosening his tie. He shrugged out of his button-up shirt to reveal a torso split in two, a lopsided gash of a mouth, lipless, rimmed in long, sharp teeth. He bent over me, the giant mouth gaping wide, and as it enveloped me, I could only think:

Fuck. I wish I'd never done peyote. Not even once.

10

Thoughts and Prayers

"Our thoughts and prayers are with the victims of the recent Strickland School Shooting and the tragic loss of life that occurred so recently on the heels of—"

Mackenzie's mother switched off the car stereo. The abrupt silence made Mackenzie's ears buzz, a kind of underwater sound.

"You don't have to go to school today," her mother said, making the same offer she had earlier that morning over breakfast. "I can write you a note."

"It's fine, Mom." Mackenzie watched the brake lights of the car in front of them in the school drop-off line, mesmerized by their indecision: on, off, on, off. The car ahead of them creeped and lurched, as if making up a gap of a few inches was all that important. "Just let me out here. I can walk the rest of the way. I'll be late otherwise."

The drop-off line was longer than usual. Parents with their misplaced guilt and anxiety, Mackenzie thought—like driving your kid to school instead of sending them on the bus could somehow make a difference. Like it offered some kind of ward of protection.

Mackenzie's mother bit her lower lip. Her grip tightened on the steering wheel. "Are you sure?"

"It's fine," she repeated, and rolled her eyes. Adults were hopeless. "We're not even doing anything half the day. Just that big assembly thing."

She didn't wait for a response before pushing open the door. A light dust of snow had stuck to the dead winter grass of the school lawn, but the sidewalk was just damp slush. She picked her way carefully up the incline toward the school building, the honking and farewells and idle chatter from the drop-off line fading into so much background noise.

~*~

The statue had already been erected in the small courtyard that divided the main school building from the gymnasium. It was covered, the heavy cloth draped over it like some awkwardly wrapped gift, but the edges of the oily cloth flapped in the wind, revealing hints of bronze beneath. It was impossible to tell for sure what it looked like beneath the cover, but the general shape made Mackenzie think of crucifixion, or some kind of scarecrow. But if it was a scarecrow, what was it meant to scare? Not crows, obviously: Two big ravens had settled at the top of the thing, perched on what might have been the head. One was calling loudly, a sound that cut through the white noise chatter of kids walking past.

Mackenzie thought of what her biology teacher, Ms. Stone, had said about ravens. "Owls might be the symbol of wisdom," she'd said, "But corvids are the smartest birds." She'd gone on to explain how crows and ravens were opportunists, willing to make cross-species friendships to secure a free meal. Crows would follow wolf packs, alerting them to danger in exchange for picking at the bones of a recent kill. They used to follow soldiers into battle, too, for the same reason. They knew that people marching off to war would mean corpses later, fresh bodies with soft eyes that could be plucked out and eaten.

"It's not that they are omens of death and misfortune," Ms. Stone had concluded. "Only that they can see it coming, and turn it to their benefit."

Ms. Stone was cool like that—always telling interesting little stories and tidbits, coming up with fun things to talk about instead of always just droning on and on about mitosis and meiosis or whatever else they were supposed to be getting from the textbook. They still went over the stuff in the book, of course, but with that unspoken agreement that it was only because they had to; Ms. Stone was on their side, really, an ally against the education system bullshit.

Mackenzie glanced around the crowd, wondering vaguely if she might spot Ms. Stone here. There were teachers flanking the student body, shepherding them toward the gymnasium like dogs nipping at a flock of sheep. She didn't see her favorite teacher, but she did see Emma, her best friend, and waved at her before trying to wade through the throng of bodies, pushing against the current of the human river.

"Emma! Hey!"

Emma was cool, too, but not in a Ms. Stone way. She was almost a year older, because her birthday was in the fall. They'd met in a first semester algebra class and had bonded over how "logarithm" sounded stupid and a little dirty, and how the teacher, Mr. Iglesias, was so baffled by their shushed-up laughter every time he said the word. Today Emma wore faded jeans and an old black band t-shirt, artfully ripped like it had recently been mauled by a tiger; a bright pink cami peeked through the gaps. Her black hair was cut short at the back, with two longer strands dyed a bright blue hanging on either side of her face.

"Hey Mackenzie." Emma tucked a blue strand behind her ear and adjusted her backpack. "I hope they're not expecting us to stand around and gawk at this statue all day. It's cold as balls out here."

~*~

As it happened, no one expected them to stand outside—so that was one benefit. They gathered in the gym instead, dotting the bleachers in small clustered social groups. A bunch of the band kids had filled up the top row. It was weird to see them at an assembly out of uniform; usually they played at the pep rallies and spirit week. They'd even come in to play on the freshman orientation on Mackenzie's first day, that weird school-year prologue where only the freshmen had to come in and find their classrooms and hear about all of the clubs and activities as if they were a bunch of first-graders who had never seen a school before. But today's assembly was whatever you'd call the opposite of a pep rally. It had a funereal air.

The principal wore a gray tweed skirt-suit that made her look like the villain in a story about boarding schools. Emma elbowed Mackenzie to point it out, and the two laughed, quietly, small brief barks of amusement that died quickly in the awkward stillness in the gym. Low murmured voices. Someone coughed. Feedback whined from the microphone, Principal Mayhew holding it away from her face and frowning at it before trying again.

"Thank you all for coming," she started, which was already a pretty stupid thing to say. It's not like they had a lot of choice about it. "I know our numbers are a bit thin today. In light of recent events at Strickland, many students and their parents have chosen to stay home, and we respect that choice. Everyone must grieve in their own way. But, as a community, there is also a time and place to grieve together."

Emma was pantomiming a "blah, blah, blah" gesture with her hand, her eyes rolled up dramatically. "They're so *dumb*," she muttered, finally, disgusted, and stopped hand-puppeting to dig around in her bag instead.

"I know, right?" Mackenzie knew exactly what she meant. It wasn't a knowledge she could put into words. If asked—as she often was, her well-meaning mom always up her butt with questions about how she was *feeling* about things—she could not articulate it. But she felt it, and knew that Emma felt it, too. How stupid and useless and clueless they all were, these adults who made all of these sweeping gestures that didn't really mean anything and certainly didn't do anything.

Like. What good did it do, really, to keep your kid out of school after a shooting in the neighboring town? What was the point? It was just as stupid as thinking that driving them to school instead of sending them on the bus could make any kind of difference. A kid with a gun shot thirteen people at Strickland high school last week, and five of those kids and one teacher were dead, and Mackenzie knew it didn't matter—not like the adults seemed to think it did. It didn't matter that the school was one town over from Ridgecrest, and it didn't matter that it had been just a few days ago, and it didn't matter what kind of gun he'd had or where he got it. It didn't matter, because school shootings weren't like strep throat or head lice, something that can be caught or avoided based on contact and proximity. The shootings were a different kind of epidemic.

It was like this: When Mackenzie was five, her mother made her go to a day camp during the summer while she was at work. One day, they'd all been out in the park and the clouds had gathered overhead, a summer storm, the kind that's all booming thunder and torrential rain and is over just as abruptly as it starts. But that first peal of thunder had sent the little kids screaming and running for shelter; they'd scattered like roaches out from under some overturned rock. But then they came back, one by one, to the playground, ready to keep on playing until the rain started, at least until their camp master had the sense to round them all up and take them inside. They'd heard the thunder, and they'd screamed and ran, and the screaming made it feel like it was all over, like the danger was passed, and never mind that the next lightning bolt could be the one that killed them, never mind that the thunder was the harmless part.

And this, now, in the gym? All of this song and dance, all of these reactionary precautions, felt just enough like doing something that in a few days it would blow over. The families would still be grieving. But the *community*—what a laugh— would forget and move on, like they always did. And the adults would go on pretending that things were fine, or that their kids were so dumb they didn't know to be afraid on sunny days, like they didn't know how quick the clouds could gather when the sky was blue.

Principal Mayhew had stopped talking.

They were to have a moment of silence for the lives lost in Strickland.

People bowed their heads. A boy nearby made a rude comment,

a stab at gallows humor, but his friend elbowed him hard, told him to shut up.

On Mackenzie's left, Jayden Patterson was mumbling a prayer, his hands clasped and eyes squeezed shut. He came from a big religious family and dressed a little weird, always long sleeves and button-ups. He had two siblings at the school, too, who tried a little harder to fit in, to sand down the edges of the family strangeness, but Jayden really truly believed; he worshiped in a way too earnest to be annoying. Mackenzie even envied him a bit. She didn't know what she was supposed to be doing with the silence—what to think about, or whether to keep her eyes closed or keep looking around, furtive downcast glances.

Emma had pulled a fine-tip sharpie from her bag and was drawing on her hand, starting up the beginning of an elaborate henna design. She wanted to be a tattoo artist when she got out of school. Her mom had even agreed to get her a lip piercing on her seventeenth birthday if she still wanted one. Emma had made her write the promise down and sign it; she had it pinned up on her wall.

"Do me," Mackenzie whispered, extending a hand, and Emma took her by the wrist. Her fingers were warm, but the tip of the sharpie was cool on her skin. The smell burned her nose.

The principal was talking again. Something about moving forward. Something about a commitment to safety. Something about new policies and procedures and what have we learned.

"And that is why we've joined The Oversight Network," Principal Mayhew continued, droning on and on now, already forgetting that she was supposed to sound like she was mourning. "This program is a cross-district opportunity to focus on what matters most: The lives of each and every one of our students. And so, in conjunction with Oversight, we've chosen to erect the Overseer's Statue—not just as a memorial to those who have fallen, but as a promise that we will keep a watchful eye on those lives that are in our hands. Today, and every day, our thoughts and prayers are with the many people in this country who have lost their lives in senseless tragedies…"

Blah, blah, blah.

The talking was over, finally, and the students rose, shuffling, a crush of bodies as they started for the door so they could go out and see the unveiling of the stupid statue.

The press was already there. Somebody took a picture of the principal with a camera that had a huge flash bulb, incongruously old-fashioned. Near the statue in the courtyard, a man with a microphone stared at the big, square lens of a shoulder-mounted video camera; the cameraman counted off something on his fingers, holding them up – three, two, one, fist.

Mackenzie and Emma and Jayden Patterson joined the crowd in a lopsided semicircle around the statue, its cover no longer flapping in the breeze; the edges were crunchy with frost. The birds had gone. The sky had turned a dark, gunmetal gray, threatening more snow.

Someone in a suit tugged at the covering on the statue, and it made a "whumph" as it fell into the snow. The bronze was flat and dull under the clouded sky, no sunlight to reflect and fracture. The smooth lines, post-modern, formed a shape that might have been a person with outstretched hands and might have just been nonsense. It looked like the artist had based it on one of those pipe cleaner men you make in elementary school: A fat pole of a body, two outstretched arms swept off to the side, a big empty oval for a head—or was that meant to be a big, open, watchful eye?

"It looks like a vagina," Emma stage-whispered, and a boy

nearby laughed. Jayden's ears went pink.

In the open now, her back to the school building, Mackenzie had a fleeting awareness of how exposed they were. How easy it would be to pick them off, one two three. Wouldn't that be an ironic thing? Wouldn't that just suck? A weird, giddy sort of feeling rose up in her chest, something like fear and something like yearning and something like a sob that caught in her ribs. When you prepare for the worst for long enough, a part of you almost wants it to happen just so you won't have to worry any more.

But nobody shot them, not while they stood out in the snow in the shadow of some postmodernist's rendition of a watchful eye. Nobody died that day.

Their shooting would happen in two weeks.

~*~

Thunder.

Thunder on a clear-sky day. That was her first thought. But of course that was ridiculous; it wasn't like thunder at all. It was the sound of doors slamming, echoing down the corridor. The scrape of desks and chairs being shoved hastily across linoleum floors, slamming into doors.

The digital clock on the wall, above the flag, read 11:11.

Mackenzie thought: Had they somehow missed the announcement? Had a lockdown drill started and none of them heard?

Classmates exchanged confused glances. This was weird. They shifted in their seats, collectively unsure whether to get up.

Ms. Stone frowned. She walked away from the projector, the clicker-pointer for the presentation still in hand, and went to the door. She leaned forward, peeking out into the hall, one hand on the knob.

A pop-pop sound, like a firecracker, like popcorn in a microwave bag, and then Ms. Stone's head jerked backward. Something red splashed the door she'd been pulling shut. She crumpled, just like that, sliding bonelessly to her knees and slumped to the floor. More of the red, then, darker, blacker, spreading out in an irregular pool from her face.

Somebody screamed.

A couple of the boys moved for the door. But Mackenzie was frozen in her seat, transfixed by the sight of the teacher's blood. It was so different than on TV. Gunfire was so much quieter. Blood was so much more liquid. It made streaky drips down the classroom door.

"Mackenzie! MOVE!" Somebody grabbed her hand.

She was jerked, roughly, out of her seat. She landed hard on her hands and knees, crouched down on all fours, but that wasn't right. That wasn't what they were supposed to do yet; they were supposed to help move all the chairs in front of the door. That was the next part of the drill. But there was no time. The boys were struggling with a filing cabinet. They didn't know how to barricade the door with Ms. Stone's body slumped down in front of it, half-in, half-out. They were arguing in quick, frantic voices.

A dark shape then, a silhouette in the doorway. Mackenzie stared through the forest of legs—student legs and desk legs and chair legs—and her gaze traveled up his dark pants and his dark hoodie and she saw his face but she didn't see anything, not really. It might as well have been a blank oval. Like Slenderman. Like that stupid statue outside. It didn't matter whether or not he had a face because he had a gun, he had a gun he had a *GUN*—!

She let out an involuntary noise and scooted backward, knocking a desk sideways as she shuffled on hands and knees away from the door.

Ms. Stone was the biology teacher, but she taught chemistry too, for the seniors, and the back part of the classroom was a chemistry lab with tables and cabinets and a big free-standing shelf filled with equipment. Mackenzie crawled toward it. Behind her, another pop, loud this time, horribly loud in the enclosed space of the classroom. Her ears began to ring. They echoed the flat, static hum in her brain, her thoughts making the sound a TV makes right after it's switched off. A girl was screaming. Mackenzie thought: *You're supposed to be quiet. That's what we're supposed to do. Be quiet.*

But it was too late to be quiet. Another gunfire. The screaming stopped.

Mackenzie ducked behind a lab table. Her heart hammered in her chest, and she could hear the blood rushing in her ears, a whoosh-whoosh beneath the ringing. It was deafening. How was she supposed to hear anything? How was she supposed to know where the gunman was? What if he was behind her? What if he was standing right behind the table, what if he was about to bend down, what if—

The tables were in pairs, two identical rows, and across the aisle she could see Jayden Patterson pressed up tight against the wood. His knees were pulled up to his chest and his hands were clasped and his eyes were screwed up tight. Tears leaked from the corners. His lips moved in a murmuring prayer.

Emma. Where was Emma? She had English this period. The classroom was at the far end of the hall. Which direction had the gunman come from? She squirmed to pull her phone out of her pocket.

A crazy idea threatened to surface in Mackenzie's subconscious, an urge so strong she almost stood and ran. But before her brain could give the command, her body froze her in place. Fight or flight, Ms. Stone had taught them, fight or flight or freeze. *Isn't it funny*, Ms. Stone had said, *how the games we play as children are all about hiding and running? That's survival instinct. That's what it means to be an animal, a part of the living world.*

But Ms. Stone's voice was only in her head now; it would only ever be in her head.

Her vision started to swim and she blinked rapidly. There was no time for tears. She had to stay sharp. She had to—

The phone screen lit up. A message. She'd forgotten she was holding it. When the text came through, the time came with it, and she stared uncomprehending at the number. That couldn't be true. It said 11:13.

Two minutes? It couldn't possibly have been just two minutes.

But her gaze darted down to the message. She ran her thumb clumsily over the button to unlock the screen. It filled with texts.

Emma: What's going on?

Emma: Is this real? Is this really happening?

Emma: Answer

Emma: Please tell me your battery died or

Emma: Plz

Pop. Shatter. A bullet hit the free-standing shelf, and it spun with the force. Beakers and test tubes scattered, shattering as they hit the tile. A stray fragment of glass struck Mackenzie's cheek and she flinched, squeezing her eyes tight, instinctive gesture. Her phone was in her hands. She should call the police. Had anyone done that yet? Were they coming? She should tell Emma she was okay. She should call her mom. She should—

~*~

Principal Mayhew's pants were smeared with blood.

Her back ached, too, down low at the juncture of her hip. She knew she'd be too stiff to move by the morning, once her muscles had seized up.

The sun hid in the sky, buried behind flat gray clouds. Ravens called, their harsh voices stark against the hush. A light snow had begun to fall, fat wet flakes fluttering lazily toward the ground. The slush that had accumulated on the grass was pinkish from the blood, mixed up and swirled with the brown-black mud and clumps of sod. The landscapers would be angry come springtime. Dragging the bodies out across the lawn had wrecked the grass.

The statue stood mutely in the heart of the courtyard. The light was too diffused to cast a proper shadow, so it looked flat, like it had been drawn in place rather than erected as a physical object. The bodies stacked in front of it were a dark, shapeless mass, impossible to tell where one ended and the next began. A mix of clothes and shoes and tangled limbs and blood, all that blackening, congealing, disgusting blood. The scent of it, that fetid coppery stench, overwhelmed the principal's senses. She thought she might be sick.

The others clustered around her. Faculty. Police. Even the mayor, his pristine suit looking out of place among the grime.

They formed a circle around the statue and its pile of sacrifices, linking hands.

The Overseer's great lidless oval eye seemed somehow to blink. Light flickered from within, a purple-black glow the color of galaxies, a light that held innumerable stars.

"Overseer. Mighty old god N'ramagath, we come with our

offering of blood. We give you our thoughts and our prayers and our children that you might hear our plea," the mayor said.

"Thoughts and prayers," the assembled chanted, an echoing response.

"We feed your hunger, that we might prosper. We wait for your holy sign."

"Thoughts and prayers." A rhythmic echo, the steady pulse of the ritual's power.

How many more? Principal Mayhew thought. How much longer until it would work? How many sacrifices would it take for this to, at last, be complete—for the summoning to at last be finished?

"Thoughts and prayers!" they chanted again, as the sky darkened overhead, as the deep pulsing violet light within that awful cosmic eye brightened.

"Guide us! Show us the path to your glory and salvation! Tell us what we must offer!"

And from the depths of that unblinking, awful eye, a rumbling sound, the tearing apart of worlds. A single great and terrible word: "**MORE**."

The light went out. The assembly bowed their heads, their hands unclasped, dropping to their sides.

"N'ramagath has spoken."

It would take time, and more blood would be spilled. But more Overseers could be erected. The great eye would soon stand watchful over schoolyards and shopping malls, concert fields and movie theaters. And, in time, it would finally be sated. Satisfied. Pleased. It would have to be. And then, surely—surely—the rewards would be worth the sacrifices.

11

Home for the Holidays

NO ONE SHOULD BE ALONE FOR THE HOLIDAYS, the billboard intoned from the side of the highway.

It was one of those black ones with white letters, like the fundamentalists put up, but if there was a phone number on there to call and learn about Jesus, I was driving too fast to see it.

The next sign was more cheerful, all red and green: WELCOME TO HOLLYVALE!

The radio dropped signal, sound going fuzzy at the edge of its broadcast area. A moment later, a Christmas carol came over the radio with a crackle of static, coming out half-garbled. Something felt weird about the song, and it took me a minute to realize the words were wrong, like someone had added an extra verse:

Wherever you go for the holiday,
You cannot afford to be alone
You deserve to be happy, and the only way
Is for you to open up your home.

"Weird remix, but okay," I said aloud, to dispel the creepy feeling crawling up my back. I quickly switched off the car stereo. "They'll make anything into a Christmas song these days. I'd rather have Mariah Carey, thanks."

The rest of the journey passed in silence, just the sound of the highway bumping along beneath my tires, the wind whipping outside my window when I rolled it down for a cigarette.

~*~

The town of Hollyvale got its name from its founder, John Holly. When I was a kid, the place was like any other small town in Nowhere, USA—half-vacant shopping centers stitched together along the main drag, "Building for Lease" signs in every other boarded-up window, the usual collection of Wal-Marts and Taco Bells. But since I left for college, the place has changed. Like most Christmas-named towns—North Pole, Alaska or Bethlehem, Pennsylvania or Christmas, Michigan, I guess Hollyvale leaned hard into the Christmas Spirit. Maybe it helped with tourism. In just a couple years, the town had transformed into something unrecognizable.

Main Street looked like one of those chintzy Christmas villages that people buy for their mantels, rows of buildings done up with twinkling lights and gingerbread-icing trim, cone-shaped trees outside, a blanket of snow across every roof and awning. And since Hollyvale is one of those small towns that lives right on the highway, recycled Rt. 66 Americana, it was impossible to get anywhere without taking the forced-slow drive down Main, traffic lights at every block pretty much forcing me to stop and look at the light-wrapped trees, the tinsel snowflakes, the winter scenes painted in storefront windows.

They'd even erected a wrought-iron archway where the shops ended, where Main turned back into country highway for a little while. Die-cut letters spelling HOLLYVALE, holly leaves and berries punched out of the metal on either side. It looked like the gate to a cemetery.

~*~

I underestimated traffic and got to Mom's house an hour later than I'd planned.

I almost didn't recognize the place.

Mom had always liked putting up a few decorations for the season, but this year the yard looked like something out of a magazine. She'd decorated like she was afraid the spirit of Old Saint Nick himself would come down and punish her if she didn't build him a shrine. Plastic light-up Santa Clauses stood beside wicker reindeer; inflatable snow globes held a constant storm of fake snow; the tree and the hedges and the windows and the eaves hung with twinkling lights that danced and flashed like an airport runway.

Mom answered the door before I knocked.

"I heard the car," she said.

"Really getting in the Christmas spirit, huh?" I responded.

We hugged, her bony body crushing awkwardly into my soft one, and neither of us seemed to want to linger. We pulled apart quickly.

"It's something to do. With your father gone, I've had a lot of free time."

Gone. It had been almost a year and I'd never heard her say the word "dead." She always fell on euphemisms: gone, not here anymore, went away. I guess denial was her favorite stage of grief.

Then again, I was the one who stopped coming back to visit. I was the one who was too busy with my studies and work—who *made* myself too busy so I wouldn't have to come back here and face this, or her. So I guess that's a kind of denial, too. But mine started even before Dad died. I'm grieving something else.

She stepped aside so I could come in and I saw that the inside of the house was just as festively manic as the outside: lights and garland, glistening tinsel, a whole Christmas city laid out on the mantel. The house had always been small, but it was jam-packed with enough ornaments and decorations to be downright claustrophobic.

"Do you need help getting your bags?" she asked.

"Oh, no, this is it," I said, holding up the small duffel. "I packed light."

Since I won't be here very long, I didn't add. I hadn't been home for a holiday since freshman year. I couldn't bear the thought of her being all alone for her first Christmas without Dad. But I also couldn't bear the thought of staying here any longer than I had to.

"Of course. You'll be wanting to go back to your studies," Mom said.

"Only if I want to graduate." I tried to joke, but it came out flat. And then, because I didn't want to stand here and defend my life choices to my mother on Christmas Eve, I set down my duffel bag and forced on a cheerful smile. "How 'bout you give me the tour and show me what you've done with the place since I've been gone?"

~*~

"Are you seeing anybody?"

We'd managed to make polite conversation for all of fifteen minutes, the amount of time it took for her to show me every room of the house and point out all of the little decorating projects, before the dangerous topics came back around.

She set a kettle on the stove and handed me a bowl of cookie dough, rolling pin, and plastic cookie cutters shaped like stars and trees, a wordless instruction there was no point in fighting.

As it happened, I had two partners waiting at home—a polycule, if you want to be cute about it. It was an arrangement I had no intention of trying to explain tonight. It was a part of my life, like most things in the decade since I'd left Hollyvale behind, that I did not want shared, analyzed, judged or discussed.

"Nobody new in my life," I said, because it wasn't really lying and I still didn't like to lie to my mother.

"That's a shame." She clicked her tongue. "Youth is a terrible thing to waste. But I'm glad you're here. No one should be alone for the holidays."

I wouldn't have been alone. I could have been at Josie's house. I could have been out with Bastion. All three of us could have been snuggled down with a bowl of popcorn and an ironic *Die Hard* marathon.

"This is a lot of dough," I said, deflecting. "Are you trying to feed an army with cookies?"

"They're your father's favorite. Remember how we used to leave them out for Santa? He couldn't wait for you to go to bed so he could eat them."

That forced a smile. "And carrot sticks for the reindeer."

"He threw those away."

Maybe if he'd eaten a few more carrots and a few less cookies he wouldn't have had a heart attack at 45 and left me alone with you, I thought, shocking myself with my own nastiness. I didn't mean it, not really. It's just that coming home had put me on edge. Moving away from home had felt like a rocket escaping the atmosphere, all this gravity trying to pull me back. But a couple years of freedom and I was finally starting to feel grown-up, like I was starting to actually own my life. And within a few minutes of being back here, I was practically sixteen again, a surly and irritable wise-ass.

The tea kettle whistled, and Mom mixed up two mugs of cocoa, handing me one. I swallowed down my bitterness with one scalding sip.

~*~

"So what's new in your life, Mom?"

We'd retired to the living room, overstuffed with a Christmas Eve feast she'd prepared as if expecting a whole extended family. Mom, who'd always been on me about my weight, wouldn't let me up from the table until I'd had seconds, heaping them onto paper plates. Ham and potato salad and green beans. Dinner rolls with butter. Two slices of pie. It threatened to come back up, sitting uncomfortably at the back of my throat.

"I've been going to a new church," she said. "It's been helping so much. New Life Church of the Reborn."

"That's great," I said, and tried to sound like I meant it.

"It's the best thing to come to this town. Everyone is going there now. Remember Molly and James from down the street?"

I frowned. "I thought they were Jewish."

"That doesn't matter. Anyone is welcome to start a New Life!"

She tittered as if she'd said something very funny, and my gut twisted with uneasiness. I suddenly didn't want to know anything more. It didn't feel safe, somehow, this line of conversation. I thought maybe a lecture was coming my way, like she was going to try to wrangle me out of the house and off to some midnight Christmas Eve service, force my head underwater with a surprise baptism and wash off all the sin, or something.

Overreacting. A panic response from years of growing up here, but I wasn't a kid anymore. The rules had changed, if I could remember that.

Mom wasn't even paying attention. She was staring off into the distance, glassy eyed, her head some place else.

"They're really getting into the Christmas spirit now, you know. It's not at all what you'd think. I know that now."

"Mom…"

"They knew all about it in the old days," she continued, and I could hear the slurring kiss the edges of her words. "Did you know Christmas Eve used to be a time for ghosts?"

"It's in that song," I said, uncertainly. "Ghost stories. And that Dickens book."

"Yes. Now finish your cocoa. You have to go to bed or Santa won't come."

She laughed again, and I felt my insides curdle.

~*~

A noise woke me—*thump, thump*—and a sleepy part of my brain thought: reindeer? But it was fleeting, chased away when I remembered where I was. Who I was. How old.

Not reindeer. A knock at the door.

I glanced at the window, frowning at the dark. Who could be here at this hour? What could they possibly want?

I struggled free of sheets, sweaty and tangled from uneasy dreams, and pulled on a robe over my night things.

"Mom?" I called into the darkness of the hall.

No answer. But beyond, I could see light, a flickering dance of flame, and I sped up my pace, practically sprinting into the kitchen.

The table was still set for dinner, our leftovers laid out, picked-over and nestled among stacks of plates and cups, a table setting for three. Had we forgotten to put it away? I couldn't remember. But I realized, staring at it, that something else was strange. The table was covered in candles, tall wax tapers and squat votives, hurricane wicks behind glass. Laid out like an offering were all the cookies we'd baked, and more still—sugar cookies and snickerdoodles and ginger snaps, piled high in stacks tucked between candles and plates.

There were photos, too, framed snapshots. My dad stared out from a dozen frames, blank photographed eyes peering up from all directions.

At the door: *thump, thump.*

"It's time!" my mother cried, hurrying past me from the hall. She was dressed in her Sunday best, her hair curled and coiffed, done up with lipstick and eyeliner and mascara like she was ready for a night on the town. She swayed through the kitchen and toward the door like she was drunk, like she'd been hitting the wine hard after I went to bed, but her eyes were clear and focused.

It had to be well past midnight. I glanced at the clock on the stove: 3:02.

No! I wanted to yell, as Mom reached the door. *Don't open it!*

But it was too late. She flung it wide and there, filling the frame, was a looming shadow with my father's face.

If I hadn't been surrounded by so many photographs, I might not have recognized him. His flesh was sallow and waxy, pulled tight over his skull. His sunken eyes were dark and empty, his lips peeled back from yellow teeth. Most of his nose was missing; in its place was an ugly gash, twin jagged holes like something had gnawed off the skin.

A part of me wanted, more than anything, to run to him. To wrap him in a hug and apologize for leaving him behind. But a bigger part of me, the part controlling my arms and legs, was frozen with revulsion. This creature, this rotting abomination, wasn't my father. It was a cruel cosmic joke.

"You came," my mother breathed, falling forward into his arms with a quiet, choking sob. "I left the lights on for you. To guide you home. Like they said."

My father wrapped her in his arms, pulling her close, and she pressed her face into the collar of the suit he'd been buried in.

He opened his mouth wide and bent over her, digging his teeth into her neck.

Blood, thick and dark and red, painted the door frame in thick spurts.

She screamed, but not for long.

Seeing her body slump to the floor was what—finally, too late—unrooted me from where shock had frozen me in place. I reeled back from the scene of horror, looking around frantically for something, anything, I could use as a weapon.

Dad's vacant eyes rolled up, gaze locking in me. He had my mother's blood all down his front. Stepping over her, his movements erratic and disjointed like a poorly coordinated puppet, he started toward me, teeth bloody and sharp and flashing in the candlelight.

For a year, I had lived with regret that my last memory of my dad would be his dead face in his casket. That I hadn't come to visit more before he died. But I'd trade anything to get that memory back, because now whenever I think of him all I'll be able to see is his bloody chin, his vacant eyes, his sharp yellow teeth.

"What the fuck," I whispered, and my shaking hands found the handle of a skillet in the sink. I pulled it out, sudsy and dripping with scraps of soggy food, and held it in like a bat. Ready to swing. "What the fuck."

Dad lumbered close. I dodged sideways, his outstretched arms just brushing past me as I feinted left. I spun around and swung the frying pan at the back of his head, full force. CRACK! The force of the collision rattled through the bones of my hand. I dropped the skillet and ran for the door.

Keys, keys. I needed the keys. Mine were in my bag in my room—but Mom's were on a hook by the door, and I didn't think she'd be needing her van anymore. I grabbed for them desperately, jumping over Mom's body on the floor, but something caught my ankle and I pitched forward, landing hard on my elbows. I kicked my foot, looking back to see Mom, her hand wrapped around my ankle, her eyes blue-white and milky. Her mouth yawned open.

I kicked her in the face and crawled forward, heaving myself to my feet and stumbling down the porch steps.

"Don't go!" Mom's voice, wet and gurgling from the blood, called out from the door behind me.

"No one," Dad's voice, a dry rasp, joined hers. "Should be alone for the holiday."

I dared to look back at them from the driveway, just one last glance. Dad's eye had popped out from the force of the impact to his skull; it dangled onto his cheek. Mom's head lolled sideways, the muscles torn from the bite no longer able to hold it upright. They were no longer my parents. If they had ever been my family, they were not anymore.

Home was my apartment overlooking the city. My family was Josie and Bastion and the cats. The friends I've made at school and work. The life I'm carving out for myself, hard-won. It's whatever I want it to be.

And if I stayed here one more minute, I'd never make it back.

I jumped into the van.

I reversed into the street and peeled away, tires screeching. Ahead, moving in a herd of helter-skelter bodies, were a dozen corpses. They shambled up the street toward me, eyes trained on the glow of Christmas lights, those homing beacons that guide planes home to land.

I gritted my teeth and hit the gas, braced for impact. Bodies thumped wetly off the bumper, bouncing away. The van rocked side to side as the tires rolled over one lump in the road; in the rearview, the corpse looked up from the street, half-flattened, and stared after me with an expression of vague surprise.

I blew through all the lights on Main Street. There was nobody around to stop me. Hollyvale belonged to the dead now. The town was crawling with corpses—some old and decayed, some fresh and bleeding. Red splattered over the snow like stripes on a candycane.

The van stereo came on by itself, a raspy, staticky voice crooning:

No one should be alone for the holidays,
No body should be forced to rot alone
If you want to live forever in the Dark Lord's grace
Call upon your loved ones, bring them home....

12

The Observer Effect

Jacob Murray was six years old the first time he suspected he could make things happen just by thinking about them.

It was Christmas Eve, and he'd made a plan for catching Santa Claus in the act. Tommy Whitmore at school had declared earlier in the week, just before the break, that Santa wasn't real and that believing otherwise was babyish. That made Ellie Rose cry, and it ignited a fierce playground debate at recess.

"Of course Santa's real," Jacob had insisted, logically. "Where else do the presents come from?"

"Parents, duh." Tommy, who was almost a year older than the other first-graders after having been held back a grade, was a self-proclaimed expert in many worldly topics. "You really are dumb."

Jacob had a cheap camera he'd begged for at the thrift store where his mother bought his school clothes at the beginning of the year. He would stay up, sneak out of his bedroom and camp in the hall. The first sound of jingling bells or reindeer hooves and he'd be ready to catch the fat man on camera, and then he'd have photographic evidence that he could push under that stupid Tommy's nose when school started again after the holiday.

So he waited, scratchy-eyed and irritable as the night wore on without any sign of Santa. He finally fell asleep just as the first gray light of dawn started to creep in around the curtains, and his parents found him there, sleeping in the hallway.

"What were you doing down there?" his mother asked, plucking him off the ground and peeling carpet lint from his pajamas.

He explained, and she chuckled. "He won't come if you're watching."

His gifts that year had been disappointing—all clothes and books, none of the toys he had asked for—and he'd felt with a sour kind of certainty that he knew exactly why. It wasn't that stupid Tommy Whitmore was right; it was that Santa was a test of faith, and watching for him had broken some sacred contract that Jacob hadn't realized he was part of.

~*~

As he grew older, Jacob eventually accepted that Santa Claus was indeed a fiction, and that his sixth Christmas was—like his thrift store attire—the product of his family's poverty, not the breaking of any magical vows. He knew this rationally, but it did not stop the quiet, creeping voice at the back of his mind that wondered: *If you had just stayed in bed like you were supposed to, would you have gotten everything that you wanted?*

It wasn't just the Santa thing, either.

He'd gotten in the habit of waiting by the door for his dad to come home from work every day, sitting on his knees and peering through the window over the back of the couch, watching for the company work truck to roll up. Every day like clockwork, his dad came home at 5:30, and Jacob would scramble to reach the door before his father could open it, flinging it wide so his dad's grease-stained hands wouldn't have to touch the knob.

He did this every day, reliably, for the year between his eighth and ninth birthdays. Then, just after he turned nine, he'd been spending the afternoon with Cassie Parker, who had a brand new PlayStation he'd been aching to try out. They'd been so caught up on the fighting game that he lost track of time. When he realized, it was already 5:32, and he scrambled to grab his backpack and run home as fast as he could. He was panting and gasping by the time he made it, doubled over at the foot of the driveway, but he was too late.

There were strange cars parked in the drive, and his dad's work truck was nowhere to be seen. His mom was crying. She couldn't explain what had happened, and he didn't figure out the whole story for hours, not until his aunt had pulled him aside to ask if he understood and to explain, as gently and patiently as possible, that there had been an accident on the job site, that his dad had died and two other workers had been very badly hurt, and it was nobody's fault but those cost-cutting assholes who ran the place without regard for their worker's safety.

But Jacob knew, then, deep down, that it was his fault. He knew, in that place that's too primal for logic, that he had broken that sacred pact with the universe once again.

In the years that followed, though he would not consciously admit to it, he learned to live by two basic observations: that good things would never appear if you looked for them, and that tragedy could only be averted by vigilance.

~*~

"Dude, stop doom-scrolling and get into the game. It's your turn to shoot." Jordan plucked the cell phone from Jacob's hand, frowning at the screen. "I'm confiscating this from you for the evening. It's not healthy to read all this news all the time."

"Yeah, man, it's downright hazardous to your health." Donald handed the pool cue to Jacob, clapping him heartily on the back.

Jacob accepted the cue and slowly circled the pool table, looking for an easy shot to take. Someone had gotten the jukebox to play "Don't Stop Believin'," and a group of rowdy drunks were singing along, loudly and out of key, their voices cutting through the general din of bowling balls and chatter.

He was a grown man now, with a programming job and a small but decent set of friends, and he had mostly buried his childhood worries about contracts with the universe. But watching Jordan slide his phone in a hoodie pocket filled him with unease all the same. In the think pieces, people called it FOMO—fear of missing out. But Jacob didn't think that was quite accurate. That made it sound like he was waiting on tenterhooks for an invitation to a party, when really it was more like checking every few minutes to be sure the world wasn't ending outside the walls of this bowling alley.

But he didn't ask for his phone back. He made his shot, sinking the 15-ball in the corner pocket, and Alexis came back just in time with a pitcher of beer and four glasses, and Jacob managed to swallow down his anxieties with a few long, foamy gulps.

~*~

Jacob woke on his couch with an awful, throbbing headache that made it feel like his brain was a swollen, pulsing mass inside a skull two sizes too small. He must have gotten a ride home with someone, or called for an Uber, but he had no recollection of doing it. He didn't remember much of anything about the later parts of the night.

The living room lamp was on, but it was still dark outside, so he couldn't have been out for long. In the dim light, squinting against the throbbing in his skull, he almost didn't see the figure sitting in the room across from him.

But his eyes regained focus, and he shot upright, yelping in surprise.

"Don't be afraid," a voice said, in a low, resonant hum.

Do not be afraid. Wasn't that what angels always said when they appeared in the Bible? The stranger in Jacob's living room did not look like any angel he'd ever heard of.

He was roughly human-shaped, although quite short, slender and with a complexion so smooth and even that it looked like latex. He was dressed strangely, like something from a fever dream combination of *Mad Max* and *Doctor Who.*

"What the fuck!" Jacob scrambled to his feet and felt woozy, the room spinning helter-skelter beneath his feet. He fell back to the couch, swallowing down an urge to vomit. "Who are you? How did you get in my house?"

He pawed at his phone in his pocket to call for the police, but the screen was dead. Out of battery.

"I'm sorry to alarm you, but there is little time to explain," the stranger said, adjusting his scarf. "I am from your future. I've come to warn you."

Jacob blinked. Dragged a hand over his face. Rubbed his eyes vigorously several times. The man was still there, still wearing eccentric layers of clothing: a suit vest, a scarf, a leather jacket with studs on the shoulder, knee-high leather boots. He was still watching Jacob with beady, intent little eyes and still glancing away anxiously every few minutes to check one of the several pocket watches adorning his person.

"I'm still drunk. I'm dreaming. This is a hallucination."

"Please, Mr. Murray, I need you to listen and understand. There isn't much time." The stranger folded his leg primly over his knee and leaned forward in the chair. "Are you familiar at all with the Heisenberg Principle?"

Now Jacob *knew* he must be dreaming. "Like the guy in *Breaking Bad*?"

The stranger pulled a handkerchief from one of his many pockets and began cleaning his wire-framed spectacles. His eyes looked smaller without them, barely more than black dots in the masklike smoothness of his face. He exhaled a beleaguered sigh. "No. All right. What about Berkeley's theories of immaterialism?"

Jacob shook his head. A belch rumbled up, tasting like stomach acid and hops. Liquid sloshed unpleasantly in his guts, choppy like stormy seas.

"The point is, it all comes down to the observer effect." The stranger paused to clear his throat. His eyes narrowed as he swallowed, sinking down into their sockets, the skin stretching strangely over his cheeks as though a rubber mask were being pulled taut. He replaced his glasses on the bridge of his nose. His face reshaped itself into normal proportions. "The long and short of it is that *watching* changes everything. The whole world is just full of possibilities, but as soon as somebody comes along and sees them and documents them and tells the world about it, those possibilities get nailed down as realities."

The tumultuous sea in Jacob's gut froze, his innards changed to ice.

"You know what I'm talking about, don't you? You're special,

Mr. Murray. You have a gift. You've always known, on some level, that your perceptions were the key to shaping this world. Haven't you?"

Jacob nodded, not trusting himself to speak.

"The problem, you see, is that everything that happens now is being observed—and everything that is being observed is happening. Ideas have power. For thousands of years, that didn't really matter. But now everything that can be imagined, every configuration of possibilities, is being spoken into existence and powered up by belief. And for reasons that should be apparent, that is not at all sustainable. One look at your world shows what happens when observations are allowed to run amok. It's chaos. Political scandals, plagues, civil unrest, aliens, clowns and obelisks and all the rest—disasters are being dreamed into existence at a rate faster than reality can possibly hold them."

Jacob finally found his voice. "But why me? Why are you telling me this?"

"We've been watching you. We've seen the way you lose sleep, tossing and turning and thinking about all of the sadness in the world. We've watched the hours you've spent on the internet, the news stations, the public access radio. You consume headlines the way a gourmet samples a tasting menu. You, Mr. Murray, are a connoisseur of disasters."

If they had been watching him do these things, hadn't they—by their own logic—been causing him to do it? Jacob wanted to ask, but didn't want to seem like a smart-ass. Beneath the stranger's amiable dishevelment, Jacob thought he could sense something else, something reptilian and steely. Dangerous. He didn't want to find himself on the wrong side of it. So instead, he asked, "Why me? Out of all the people in the world, why me?"

The stranger laughed. "Did you…did you really think you were the only one?" He removed his glasses again, swiping at his eyes. Jacob thought he saw the skin ripple and fold around his mouth, like a mask bunching and slipping, but the effect was gone as soon as he'd noticed it. "Goodness, no. But you are one of the special ones. We're reaching out to the others, as well. We hope it will be enough to stem the flow in time to avert disaster."

The stranger put his glasses back on, straightening them, and then consulted one of his watches.

"And with that, Mr. Murray, I fear I must leave you. There are many others we must approach today."

"Wait!" Jacob surprised himself with the panic in his voice. "I don't…I still don't understand what it is you want me to do?"

"Stay away from the news," the stranger said. "Stop being an observer. We'll follow up if we need anything further."

The stranger stood, and Jacob felt a strange shift in pressure, as if the air around him had become impenetrably thick. It squeezed his brain, a low humming sound starting deep in his skull, and he shut his eyes and grimaced against the almost unbearable pressure, worried that his breath would catch in a collapsing chest, worried that his skull would crumble under the pressure of his headache.

When he opened his eyes again, the stranger was gone. His room was dark and cold and empty, save for the discarded fast food wrappers that littered the table and floor.

He took two aspirin and went to bed.

~*~

Jacob's headache was gone by morning, and he woke mostly ready to write off the prior night's conversation as a strange but vivid alcohol-fueled dream, nothing more than penance for going out on a work night. The details had already begun to blur by noon, and as he opened his work laptop and started sorting through emails, it was all but forgotten.

All the same, he left his phone off the charger that day. Instead of turning on the news as background noise as he usually did, he put on some music.

If there were any impending disasters in the world, he did not know about them. It felt good.

~*~

"You? Going cold turkey off the news? I don't believe it," Jordan teased, stuffing his lunch bag in the break room fridge.

"Hand to god. I'm one week news-free now. No talk radio. No social media. It feels amazing."

"I've been doing that, too," Alexis said, and their eyes met briefly. He thought he saw something there, a flash of deeper understanding, some knowing expression passing between them. "A whole digital detox. It's nice."

"I'll add that one to my apocalypse bingo card," Donald said.

It was the last time they spoke together like that, the four of them, before the office shut down, a two-week quarantine that stretched into an indefinite work-from-home arrangement. Jacob missed the chatter, but found it was easier to stay disconnected while working from home, out of earshot of viral cat videos and lunchroom political debates.

He deleted his social media accounts, but he kept Alexis's phone number saved. Just in case.

~*~

When he went to the grocery store, he found signs plastered up in the door: No Mask, No Entry.

Outside, a line had gathered, spaced out along markers on the pavement. People wearing surgical masks turned to glower at him, and he retreated to his car. He hadn't realized it was getting this serious.

His hand itched, that old familiar urge, and he gave in this time. In the grocery store parking lot, he pulled up his phone browser and sought out the infection rate. Death statistics. A pile of news articles: mask mandates, conspiracy theorists, state-wide lockdowns. He drove home when he realized he'd been reading in the parking lot for an hour, but back at the house, he couldn't stop. He lay in bed and read for hours.

By the end of the night, when he refreshed the death statistics page, the fatalities had doubled.

~*~

"We are very disappointed in you, Mr. Murray."

The stranger stood at the foot of his bed, two other similarly dressed figures flanking him. The rest of the room was darkness. When the stranger spoke, Jacob could not see his lips move.

He struggled to sit up, but his body wouldn't listen; he lay as if paralyzed, staring up at the trio of strangers who loomed over him.

"You were doing so well. But I'm afraid you're not taking this seriously. Thousands are dead now."

That wasn't me, he tried to say, but found that his tongue, like the rest of his body, was frozen stiff; it stuck to the roof of his mouth, stubbornly pressed to his teeth. *I didn't do anything.*

Light caught the stranger's eyes; they flashed yellow-white, then blinked and were gone.

~*~

"It's like everybody's lost their sense of object permanence." Jacob speared a chunk of orange-glazed chicken on the end of his chopstick, popping it into his mouth. He frowned at his bowl of noodles. "Like once you drop off social media, you just stop existing. Nobody even calls anymore."

"I know what you mean," Alexis said. "You know my sister had a baby last week and nobody even bothered to tell me? They just assumed I knew. Everyone assumes everyone knows everybody's business now. Because it's on Facebook. Isn't that fucked up?"

Her image in the video chat lagged momentarily, the sound distorting, and Jacob waited for the feed to right itself before he spoke.

"Do you ever think that, maybe, if people stop talking to you, stop acknowledging you, maybe you'd just disappear?"

Alexis shifted her weight, eyes going narrow. Hesitantly, "In a, like, suicide-y way?"

He shook his head. "No, no, nothing like that. I mean. In a literal sense. Do you think if nobody thinks about you or talks about you or looks at you anymore, you stop existing?"

"I think that problems don't go away when you ignore them," Alexis said. She hesitated. "Jake, if there's something else going on in your life that you need to talk about..."

"It's fine. It's nothing." A steady pressure was building in his skull, an atmospheric throbbing that felt entirely too familiar. He waited for the edges of reality to blur, for the air to shimmer like a heat mirage, but it did not happen. The strangers did not appear. "I just. I'm trying my best, you know? I'm trying to do what they asked me to do, and they keep saying it's helping, but how would I know? If I'm not allowed to look, how do I know it's working?"

"What are you talking about? What *who* asked you to do?"

"The strangers. They come at night and they tell me..." He trailed off, looking for that spark of familiarity in her eyes, that gleam he'd seen that day in the break room. That hint that she was one of the special ones, like him. But it was hard to read an expression through a video chat. It was hard to know what she was thinking across the distance.

"Jake, I don't know what you're saying. You're scaring me."

"Forget it. It's nothing."

"I should get going." She glanced away, looking at something off-screen. "And you should...maybe you should talk to somebody, man. Take some time off work. Get some sleep."

"I'm sorry." He realized, too late, what was happening, but he was frozen to his seat. "I said something weird, I didn't mean to..."

"No, no, it's fine. Just...take care of yourself, all right?"

~*~

He left a few voicemails, but Alexis never returned them, and he gave up after a few days. With no one left to talk to, he let his phone plan lapse. It sat like a dark, glass brick on his nightstand, an artifact of a previous time.

Maybe, he thought, she was testing his theory after all. Maybe she wanted to see if he'd disappear.

~*~

The sirens woke him, some nights.

He couldn't say for certain when it had started or when they had escalated. But he was aware that there were more now than there had ever been. He was certain that, for the several years he had lived in this house, an ambulance or firetruck screaming past in the night had been a rarity. Now they were a nightly occurrence, sometimes more than once, and he often lay in bed and wondered about them.

Is this it? Is this the apocalypse they tried to warn me about? Or is something else coming? Something worse?

Without the distraction of his devices, he had nothing to take his mind off the speculation. And he wondered, listening to the squeal of tires and persistent caterwauling of the night's fourth ambulance, whether listening and counting was making them proliferate.

The next morning, he ordered earplugs and a sleep mask, had them shipped overnight.

When he slept again, he thought he could hear a whisper in his skull, breath skipping past the earplugs to say softly and clearly: *Good work. Now just a little bit more*

~*~

When the lay-offs came, Jacob was first in line. It didn't surprise him. Profit loss meant budget cuts, and budget cuts meant staffing—and his work had been slipping for months since he'd been working from home. Truthfully, he was relieved. Working was a distraction from preparation.

He added padding to the windows and around the seams of each door in his house, blocking out the light and sound. He shut off his internet; there was no need for it anymore. When he wasn't working on the house, he read, or did puzzles. He slept often, and woke sometimes with tears in his eyes and a throbbing head, though he no longer remembered his dreams.

He had his delivery drivers leave groceries and takeout on the front step, too afraid to talk to them for fear the small-talk might make him learn something else about the world that he wasn't meant to know.

~*~

The electricity went out sometime overnight.

He woke to the sound of alien stillness and silence in his home, the buzzing current dead now in its wires. He went to the breaker and flipped it with no response. Had he paid the bill? His memory was fuzzy. Without a phone or internet, getting the bills out on time was harder than it used to be. But he thought he remembered having written a check. He was almost certain that had been this month.

He hesitated, a moment of weakness, and lifted the corner of his bedroom curtain to peek outside. He was met with darkness. The lights in the neighborhood were out. Curiosity stirred in him, and he fought an urge to rip the curtain away, to press his face to the glass or to go outside for a better look—but he swallowed it down. Looking outside was risk enough already.

Something moved outside, passing in front of the window. A figure, short and oddly dressed, its eyes narrow slit in the rubbery, taut skin of its face. It slowly angled its head toward him and he quickly pulled away from the window, pressing the corner of the curtain back with a tack, hoping the stranger had not seen him peeking.

~*~

"You've done very well, Mr. Murray," the stranger said, his face close to Jacob's in the darkness of his waking dream.

"You've done everything we asked for," the second stranger said, looming behind his friend.

Their faces were strange and contorted, flesh-toned rubber pulled into the shape of bird heads, eyes narrow slits over orange eyes with upright, rectangular pupils. Their mouths stretched wide, toothless and fleshy. Jacob didn't know how he had ever mistaken them for people.

"You've been our star pupil."

"Rest now. It will all be over soon."

~*~

The lights never came back on.

Outside, muffled by the foam padding over his doors and windows, he could just make out a distant sound like screaming. He thought he could see flickers of light, like a strobing searchlight, its glow rising and falling rhythmically through the frosted glass at the top of his door. He had forgotten to nail cardboard over it.

Don't look, he thought. *Don't look, and it will be over quicker.*

Don't look, and it won't be real.

Something rattled his doorknob. He saw it jumping in place, the subtle wobbling of the brass knob as someone or something jiggled it from the outside. He heard thumping, scraping, against the wood. A low, rasping moan, like a thing snarling deep in its throat.

Would it be acknowledging the thing outside to barricade the door?

If he opened it right now, what could he do to stop it? What power did he have, beyond that one skill, his one terrible superpower?

He leaned heavily against the door, feeling it thump on its hinges, the wood rattling in its frame. He tried hard not to think of what was on the other side.

If you imagine it, you'll summon it, he thought, and gritted his teeth.

His lifetime had prepared him for this moment. A lifetime of watching and checking and obsessing and worrying, all boiled down to this single impossible task.

He only needed to outlast the terrible thing, whatever it was. Needed only to keep that door closed, and he could save the world. That was what the strangers had meant, wasn't it? That was what they had asked him to do.

When Pandora was given her box of monsters, had the strangers been the ones to give it?

When Lot's wife looked back on Gomorrah, was it the strangers who saw her turn to salt?

When Jacob's father died in the oilfield, had the strangers been there, too?

He squeezed his eyes shut and willed his breath to steady.

~*~

Jacob didn't think it would be possible to fall asleep, but he woke with a miserable ache in his neck and a tightness in his shoulders, searing pain from a long night spent huddled against the closed door.

It was impossible to know how long it had been, whether it was day or night outside. Inside his house, every hour was the same shade of dark.

He groaned and struggled to his feet, pressing his ear against the door. Silence. No more muffled screams, no more groaning and chuffing and pounding. He touched his hand to the knob, and breathed in a long, steadying breath.

He undid the deadbolt. Swung the door open.

And was greeted by nothing.

It wasn't just the darkness of the power being knocked out, stars smothered in a late-night sky. It was an unfinished nothing, a void, a broad expanse of emptiness that shimmered and danced at the edges of his vision, like the after-image of staring at the sun. The houses across the street—gone, eaten by darkness. The trees and street signs and skyline, vanished, wiped away like lines of errant code.

"Thank you."

The stranger's voice brushed past his ear like a hot, dry wind. Jacob turned, numb and shaking, to see a dozen of the creatures filling up the room, their beaklike faces split into wide, toothless smiles, the clocks and chains rattling on their myriad coats as they pressed in closer to him. They pushed past him, crowding on either side, bumping and jostling as they squeezed their slender bodies out the front door, stepping into the nothingness.

The world beyond his doorstep, unobserved, had ceased to exist.

And now it was a blank slate, an empty page, a history waiting to be written by monsters.

13

Sick

I was always a sickly child.

As far back as I can remember, I've had fragile health. That's how Mama put it: fragile. It meant I wasn't allowed to do a lot of things other kids could. I wasn't well enough to go to school, but I did lessons at home when I was up to it. I couldn't go spend a lot of time with the neighbor kids, because they might give me some germs, or I might give them some, I'm not real sure which. Both, maybe.

I didn't spend much time outside but I did spend a lot at the doctor's. I'd go in for tests. They'd stick me for blood and hold me overnight in hospital beds and I'd always start to feel better, for a little while, but then I was right back to the sickness, weak and feverish and too dizzy to stand, and then Mama would say it was time for a new doctor because what do these folks know, anyway.

Sometimes it ebbed and flowed, but I was never really healthy, not like other kids. It ain't so bad, though. You learn to adjust. You learn to make sick your new normal. You take up quiet hobbies, like reading and journaling. You learn to make friends in your head, since you don't get to meet many people. You develop a strong imagination. Mama always said I had a rich inner life, and I guess that's true. I spend a lot of time up in my head now.

~*~

It's just me and Mama. My dad died when I was a baby, and she's never remarried. I guess she hasn't had time, to be honest, considering the illness. My health takes up all her time, between the doctors and the homeopathic treatments and the home-school lessons and the time she spends nursing me when I'm too weak to get up out of bed.

So we're very close, me and Mama, and she's made so many sacrifices in her life to try and make things better for me.

We moved around a lot when I was little. We were always looking for new doctors and specialists, or trying different environments to see if my medical issues might be environmental. One doctor thought it might be an allergy issue, or some kind of sensitivity to certain chemicals in the house like the paint or the insulation or somesuch, so Mama packed us up and we moved several times.

With all the moving and the sickness and how much Mama has to do for both of us, I guess we didn't have all that much time for school. I guess I didn't learn everything a person my age should have. Maybe if I had, I could have helped Mama sooner, before things went so wrong

~*~

We moved out recently into a place kind of "off the grid." Mama said the peace and quiet might do me good. We're also kind of far from a hospital. Some days it's bad enough I can't get out of bed, but I haven't needed the ER in a long while. Mama says there's no point, anyway. Says all the doctors have stuffing for brains.

By now, Mama says, she knows more about medicine than they do. And I believe her. She's got a whole chest of pills and tinctures and syrups and knows what to do with every one of them. She knows best, so I trust her.

But I didn't expect for her to get sick, too.

She's always been so healthy. Maybe a cold or flu sometimes, but never anything serious. So when she started to get sick, I got really worried. She got so weak she couldn't get out of bed.

But I can remember what she's always done for me, what the bottles looked like, how many pills she'd make me swallow. Lucky, I was feeling well enough to help.

At first, Mama didn't want to take her medicine. I remember feeling that way, when I was little. She was so delirious with fever that she was pushing me away, hands like claws. Begging me to stop. But I remembered how she'd make me swallow. I made sure she took her medicine, every drop.

~*~

I've had to use a lot of tricks on her, since, to make sure she takes her medicine. I'm lucky she taught me so much. I was such a difficult patient back then. I never realized how hard this was on her, fighting me all the time. But I'm just as stubborn as she is, and I know she needs the help.

So I've been sneaking medicine into her food. The tea I make for her at night. I'll slip a pill into the pocket of her cheek while she sleeps. If nothing else works and she's feeling real ornery, I'll tie her down with the silk scarves like she used to when the fevers got real bad, to keep me from thrashing around. I wouldn't want her getting delirious and trying to walk around the house in her condition.

Helping her has given me new purpose. Some days I've been so committed to helping her get better that I forget to take my own medicine. And lately, we've been running low on some things, so I've stopped taking mine so I can just focus on her.

I think having a purpose now has been good for me. I feel better than I ever have. Healthier, stronger. My symptoms have started to clear. Honestly, it almost feels like I was never sick at all.

And it's a good thing, too. Because Mama just keeps getting worse.

I'm so happy she has me here to take care of her.

14

Blackwood

"I'm sorry. I don't do this much." He flashes me an apologetic smile and, for a moment, I'm transfixed by the whiteness of his teeth and the way they contrast against the darkness of his thick beard.

"It's okay, Mr. Blackwood," I say. "I don't really do this much either."

We laugh because it's so ridiculous, and in the laughter some of the tension melts away. The silence becomes more amicable.

"Just 'Blackwood,' please. And, yes. I suppose you wouldn't. So. Do you have any qualifications? Work experience?" He glances down at the paper on his desk, the notepad that he's been intermittently scribbling on since I arrived.

The question catches me off guard. "Uh…" My eyes dart around the room—looking for an escape, or inspiration, I don't know which. The painted eyes of a self-portrait bear down on me. He's not smiling in the portrait, so his mouth is hidden behind the soft dark curls of his mustache and beard. His eyes, though, are the same: small, dark, intense and boring down on me. Caught in the double gaze of my host, I feel small and vulnerable. "I didn't know I needed experience."

"I'm just fucking with you," he says. His face splits wide with a smile that bares his too-white teeth but doesn't touch his eyes. "Look, here's the thing. I don't get out much. You get to a certain age and realize that life has passed you by. You can't really make friends or find love or any of that bullshit, so you've just got to keep doing the same things you've been doing and hope it's enough to make the kind of impact you want to make. If you care about any of that, anyway. How old are you, son?"

"Twenty-one," I lie. I look old for my age.

He gives me a shrewd look, like he's about to call bullshit, but he doesn't. Instead, he says, "Well, you're too young to understand all that, then. And I hope you never find yourself needing to. But the truth is—when you're an old, lonely sad-sack like me, you'll do just about anything for a bit of company. Even put up an ad on Craigslist. Which brings us, of course, back to our current predicament. I need a roommate, and you need a room. I'd say that's qualification enough."

"Um." I can't figure out if that means I'm accepted, and whether I really want to be. He's right about one thing: I do need a room. I've been living in a car for too long, and I'm running out of quarters for the public showers at the truck stop. I've got a job—a part-time gig, under the table, but hey, it pays for dinner—but no way to rent a place. Not unless I want to get one of those rat-trap hotels that charges by the week, the place where the homeless guys spend their window-washing money for a warm bed a couple nights a month.

So, sure, this guy is unreadable and weird, but it's not like I have a lot of other options. My Plan B is basically to live on the street until my boss figures me out, and then what happens? I don't say any of this. Instead, I just look back up at Blackwood and wait for him to keep talking.

"I think you'll find my rules amenable. I'm a fairly easy-going guy, and I generally keep to myself—which is, of course, how I ended up in this predicament. You seem like a nice young man. That's good enough for me, if it's good enough for you."

This has officially been the strangest interview I've ever had, and that's counting the one where my current boss showed up twenty minutes late and stinking of Grey Goose. Then again, he usually smells like that, so I guess that wasn't so unusual. "Okay."

Blackwood stands. He's not a very big man, but he seems to take up a lot of space regardless. Maybe it's just the huge painting behind him, the one that fills most of that rear wall. "Great. Then come with me, and I'll show you around. This house is too big, but I may as well give you a proper tour and get it out of the way."

He leads me out into the hall, which leads into another hall, and every hallway is lined with rooms. The walls are covered in paintings, and they watch us with flat eyes. The ones that have eyes, anyway. Most are of other things: hands, necks, thighs. They capture light and movement, the way muscles ripple under skin or shadows play over flesh.

Blackwood was right: The house really is too big for him. It's a sprawling Victorian home, the kind that usually gets renovated into a B&B or gourmet restaurant. A labyrinth of hallway connects an endless series of rooms. He points out necessities as he goes. "That's your room, and this one's mine. That's the sitting room over there. Sorry about the television; the cable company won't come out this far, and I didn't want to bother with a satellite. Honestly, I don't really watch much television. There's Internet, though. Dial-up—I know, I know—

but it does what you need it to do."

I don't mind. As far as I'm concerned, the house's isolation is one of its greatest strengths. The further I am from everyone else, the less likely it is that somebody I don't want to see will come looking for me.

"I don't expect you to clean more than whatever messes you make yourself," he says. "Otherwise, I would've run an ad for a maid instead."

I'm glad, because everywhere I look, I see dust or spiderwebs. It seems pretty clear that a lot of these side rooms haven't been used in ages. They're mostly filled with boxes, and many of them hold art: paintings, sculptures, drawings in ink or charcoal.

The statues are the most striking. They're life-size, or slightly larger than life-size, and made of some sort of coppery brown, marbled surface. It doesn't look like stone, but I can't quite figure it out.

"Acid-etched concrete," he says, with a smile, catching me looking. "Just as beautiful as marble, but cheaper—and easier to work with. More fluid. Malleable, and rough. It hides all sorts of imperfections."

The figures are posed in ways that conjure images of life. They occupy furniture in the vacant rooms: seated in chairs, lying in beds, standing huddled as if in conversation. They have no features, and their smooth blank faces give no emotion. Unlike everything else in most of these rooms, they are clean and free of dust.

"They keep me company," Blackwood says. From his smile, I can't tell whether he's serious.

The tour continues. Somehow, the hall circles back around, and we find ourselves near the office where we started. The rest of the lived-in rooms are huddled closely together, close to the bedrooms. The kitchen is messy and lived-in, obviously the place where Blackwood spends most of his time. There's a small table with two chairs sitting in the corner of the room. Attached to the kitchen is a dining room. It's dark and occupied only by a large table and several concrete statues. They sit around the table as if enjoying a silent meal.

"And this is my studio," he says, pointing to the last door on the tour.

The door is closed, and I notice that the knob has a keyhole, unlike most of the other rooms.

Blackwood digs around in his pockets. "Here's your spare key," he says, drawing it out and handing it to me. "It's a master key. I key all my locks the same, to spare me some time and trouble. So this will let you go anywhere you want to go—the front door, back door, garage, shed, whatever. I do ask that you stay away from my studio, though. It's full of sharp tools and harsh chemicals and expensive artwork. It's easy to get hurt break something."

"No problem," I say. "Your house, your rules."

"Our house, now," he says, with another of those face-splitting smiles. "In a manner of speaking."

~*~

Blackwood spends most of the following weeks preparing for an art exhibit. I rarely see him. He sleeps in later than I do, and when I come home from work, he's usually in his studio. Sometimes I can hear the sound of hammering or cutting or other odd noises that I can't really place. Most of the time I head back to my room without thinking too much about it. He doesn't ask me any questions, and that suits me just fine.

Mostly, I only see him at meal times. He's insisted that I help myself to the food in his house, despite my protests that I should pay for my share. "You're too thin," he'd say, looking at me with an appraising look—the way someone might look at livestock they were planning to buy. "Help yourself. You need it."

He's right, of course. I *am* too thin. I'm bony from too much time on the streets, and when I eat, I wolf down my food as if expecting someone to come and take it from me. Then again, that *was* something I had to worry about for a long time— assholes who thought it was funny to steal my lunch at school, or my dad thinking it'd be a suitable punishment to padlock all the cabinets and refrigerator.

I don't argue with Blackwood. Instead, at meal times, I try to make myself useful. I'm not a very good cook. Most of my experience comes from dunking fries in hot oil or flipping greasy patties on a grill. Still, Blackwood seems impressed.

He sits across from me and makes small talk. I try not to stare at him, so my eyes wander instead to the empty dining room. The blank faces of the statues stare back.

"I don't take them with me to shows," he tells me. "When I travel, it's only the paintings. These others—they're just for me."

I ask him to tell me about his art so I won't need to make conversation on my own. When he talks, I find my eyes always straying back to his mouth, the tangle of his beard, the fullness of his lips. I try to look at his eyes, but they're too hard, too intense, and they chase my gaze south again. So I go back to looking at the statues.

After a while, I realize he's stopped talking. I look back at him, and see that he's watching me—like I was watching him. His expression is inscrutable. "I'll be gone for a few days," he says, after the silence stretches between us. "But I'm sure you'll be fine without me."

~*~

The house is too big when I'm alone. It's obvious why Blackwood asked for a roommate. The first night that he's gone, I lay awake and listen as the house makes odd noises. It creaks and groans. I get up, once, to venture into the kitchen for a glass of water. When I walk past the studio, I hear what sounds like scratching just inside the door. Mice? I'm not sure. I pause outside to listen, but hear nothing more. After a while, I go ahead into the kitchen, get my water, and head back to bed. I don't get much sleep, and I'm exhausted by the time morning comes.

I roll out of bed and go through the motions of getting dressed for work. Somehow I know, though, in the pit of my stomach, that something is going to go wrong with it. It's just one of those mornings. I'm not even surprised when I see the flat tire. Considering how far out this place is, how rough the country road is, the flat tire seems inevitable. I don't have a spare.

I go back inside to call my boss. He answers, sounding drunk and exasperated, and tells me not to worry about it. He also tells me not to bother coming in again. It takes me a while after I hang up the phone to realize that means I've been fired.

~*~

Blackwood comes back on the third day. By then, I've worked myself up into a panic. I've got some money, but it won't last long, and I don't know when I'm going to find another job. This one was hard enough to get. I'm worried what Blackwood's going to say as soon as he figures out, so I avoid him when he gets back, but it only lasts so long before I find us both back in the kitchen, staring at each other in awkward silence over a plate of noodles.

"I, um. I might have some trouble with rent this next month," I say.

He quirks a brow.

The rest of the story spills out of me. When I'm done, my voice is trembling, and I can feel the burn creep up my cheeks and the side of my neck. I stop myself—just barely—before I say something stupid, like *Don't make me live on the street again.*

"It doesn't matter," he says, and his hand crosses the table. Stubby fingertips touch the back of my hand, creep up toward my wrist. "I don't really care about the money."

My heart thuds up into my throat. I struggle to talk around it. "I owe you something. I'll make it up to you—I'm good for it."

"I'm sure you are," he says. His fingers don't stray from my hand. "Tell you what. I could use a new model. If you really want to make it up to me, pose for me."

"A model?" I choke out. I can't imagine modeling for anything. I'm not exactly handsome. I have the kind of vague features that people quickly forget. Camouflage that's always kept me safe in a crowd. "I don't know that I'd be very good at that."

"You don't need to do much," he says, locking intense eyes upon me. "Any artist can represent a beautiful person beautifully. The art comes from drawing the extraordinary from the mundane." His fingers crawl around the inside of my wrist, brush the underside of my hand, and somehow I don't mind that he just called me mundane.

~*~

He keeps he room warm for me, but I still don't want to take off my clothes. I hold my chest, protectively, as if my hands can keep the pounding of my heart at bay.

We're not in his studio. Instead, he has me pose in his office. "The light is better," he tells me. "Softer—kinder. And it's warmer in here."

I quail under the gaze of the self-portrait on the wall. I might not mind shedding my clothes for Blackwood alone, but I can't stand the penetrating gaze from above.

"You're safe," he says. "Take it slow. Just your shirt, if that makes you more comfortable."

Stripping off my shirt shouldn't make me feel so uneasy. Other guys do it all the time—at home, at the gym. I've never been that guy, though. I try to remember the last time I was shirtless in front of someone. I can't recall. Reluctantly, I pull my shirt over my head, revealing a pale, bare torso crossed by a dozen scars—remnants of years of cutting and burning myself.

Blackwood gasps, audibly, when he sees me. "Beautiful," he says, tracing the puckered white lines of flesh with his eyes. I know he means it.

He sketches me for a long time. Occasionally, he asks me to move to capture the light. We take frequent breaks. At first I'm eager to put on my shirt again, but after a while I leave it off. I like the way he looks at me.

I model for him every day that week. He tells me stories to keep me distracted, loose. Sometimes he tells me about galleries that have shown his art, the way he handles all the details from afar. Once, he says, he found a hotel room directly across the street from the gallery and spent the day watching the crowds through the windows with binoculars. Mostly, though, he just talks about art, and most of the words blur together as I see him looking at me.

"The thing about art," he tells me, "is it's a way to make sense of life. You can take things in this world and alter them—twist and cut and shape the to be the way you want. With art, you become a god. You recreate the universe in your own image."

"Is that what you're doing to me?" I ask. "Building me in your image?"

He smiles, a shy twitch of his whiskers, and goes back to work. "Would you like that"

"Yes," I say, breathlessly, not sure anymore what I'm agreeing to.

~*~

The next session, I take off the rest of my clothes.

Like my body, my legs are covered in scars down to my knees. Blackwood draws for a while, then rises to slowly circle me. "I want to memorize every line," he says, touching my chest with a dry, stubby fingertip.

I freeze beneath his touch. I can nearly feel the heat radiating off my skin.

"When I close my eyes, I want to remember them. At night, before I sleep, sometimes they're all I can think of."

"I'm sorry," I say, because I can't think of anything else.

He laughs and moves his hand to stroke the scarred flesh of my thigh. The scar curves inward, and he follows the contour with his hand. "You're a beautiful model," he says, his hand between my legs.

Somehow, we end up on the floor together. His hands on my

body, my mouth against his skin. I feel his weight against me, on top of me, and before I can warn him that I'm a virgin —I'm not anymore.

It hurts. The pain is exquisite, like cutting, and I feel hot and cold all over. I come too soon, and apologize too much. He just laughs.

~*~

I start sleeping in Blackwood's bed. Some days, he's affectionate and loving. He stays in bed with me late in the day, or we spend time wandering the lonely grounds around his home, hands entwined. He shows me the books and articles that have been written about him, praising him as the most genius artist of the 21st Century. Nobody knows who he is, or even what he looks like, and his anonymity is at the very core of is fame. I tell him I'd never heard of him before I got to his house. We have a good laugh about that.

Other days he spends locked away in his studio for long hours. Once or twice, he's up so late working that I waken to an empty bed, and it feels more lonesome than anything has ever felt before.

I feel something for him, but I don't know if it's love. How could I? When have I ever felt love for anything—even myself?

I still model for him.

He won't show me the drawings. It's not the only secret he keeps. Before, as roommates, the closed doors and evasive answers hardly mattered to me. Now, all of it feels unbearable.

~*~

He has another exhibition, he tells me. This one will be longer than the last. It's in another state. I want to come along, but he says it's a bad idea. I'd be bored, he tells me, and besides, the media would go crazy if they found out I was with him. The famous Blackwood is so mysterious, and reporters are hungry for a scandal. They'd try to figure out all about me as a way to get close to him. That's enough to stop me from asking again.

Besides, as he packs the van I realize there's some meager benefit to the empty house. I wait for him to leave, and spend some time wandering the halls. I want to kill some time, in case he comes back. He's bad about forgetting things when he leaves the house, maybe because he's so used to being home with everything he needs.

Finally, once I'm certain that he's gone for good, I make my way for his studio. I linger outside the door, listening for any odd sounds. I wait, but hear nothing—no scuffling, no scratching. Still, I cannot avoid the curiosity that rises up in me. What is he doing in there all alone for so many hours? I've helped him load up his truck for two exhibits now and none of the artwork came from inside.

It's a master key.

His words echo in my mind, a memory that bubbles to the surface. I don't know why, but the thought is suddenly exhilarating. My heart begins to pound, and my fingertips tingle.

I head back to my room to retrieve the master key.

I catch a glimpse of myself in the mirror and I'm surprised by what I see. I'm heavier than I was, more solid. I look older, too, and some of my softness has been sculpted into hard angles. I've got a full beard now—so much like his.

Rebuilding the world in your own image.

I take the key and head down to the studio. I spend a breathless moment outside, certain that the key won't fit, and then the lock clicks and I step inside.

Several odors assault my nose at once: the smell of decay, embalming fluid, acid, concrete.

It takes my eyes a minute to adjust to the gloom of the darkened room. Once they do, my eyes are drawn to a wall of photographs, each pinned haphazardly, some layered one over the others. They don't make any sense. I stare at it them for a long time, too confused to be afraid.

They look like a series of progress photos. I lean in close to get a clearer look at one. It shows a cadaver—a guy about my age, maybe a little younger—propped up unnaturally on a podium. His eyes are shut, and his skin is the deathly pale of a corpse, but his arms and legs have been posed. His entire body is covered in a mesh of wire. The wire cage holds the body upright, keeps it in the right pose.

It takes me a while, but I recognize the pose. It's the same as one of the faceless statues in the dining room. My eyes flick from one photo to the next, confirming, and every pose is familiar. Boys, all of them, each one wrapped in wire and posed like a doll.

My heart catches in my throat. I want to leave—my body screams at me to run—but I can't tear my eyes away from the photos.

Above his work bench, the thing that makes my blood run cold: The drawings of me.

Sketches from every angle, every kind of light. My naked form, prostrate on the page. Drawings that I remember posing for, and some I don't—sketches of me sleeping, or loose sketches drawn from memory.

On every drawing, laid over with grids and schemes, are measurements and calculations.

How much wire to buy. How much cement to pour.

A scream catches in my throat and I back away slowly, as if afraid of waking something in the studio.

I stumble back into the hall and lock the door. The room is silent and still. The house is empty.

"I have to know," I murmur to myself. Hearing it out loud makes it seem less insane. I'm not sure what I saw inside. Maybe it's not what it looks like. Maybe there's another explanation. Thoughts racing, I go over my options. I have no car. There's a phone—but who would I call? What would I say? I know nobody. I can't imagine calling the police. *Hello, my gay lover is a famous artist and I think he's killing boys.* I can't make that kind of accusation, not without knowing for sure.

Maybe they're fake. Special effects photos. It's not that unlikely. Actors with makeup, or digital manipulations that were put together in Photoshop. Maybe he downloaded them from the internet. Maybe they weren't really the same poses as the statues in the house. There are only so many ways to pose a statue. It could all be a coincidence.

And the measurements?

I push the thought away. It doesn't make any sense. Blackwood is an artist. The most famous artist in the region, maybe the whole country. A celebrated genius of modern art. I've seen all the books about him in the study. How likely is it that he's a killer? There has to be another explanation that makes sense.

I just have to make sure. Before I do anything hasty—I have to make sure.

There's no need for silence in an empty house, but I creep away from the studio anyway. Slowly, deliberately, I make my way into the dining room, seeking out the statue from the photograph.

It's there. Just-slightly-larger than life size, features smooth and blank. I touch it—him— and the cement of his arm is smooth but porous under my touch. I rap my knuckles against it, but all I hear is the dull thud of concrete, too thick and strong to echo no matter what it may be hiding.

How can I know? How can I check?

I look around for a solution. It's too heavy to topple, and even if I could, there's no guarantees it would break when it collided with the floor. More likely, I'd have only a damaged hardwood floor to show for my troubles.

Swallowing back my fear, I make my way outside to look for a solution.

The tool shed is well-equipped. For the groundskeeper, I suppose, back when this place had a groundskeeper. Or maybe for art projects. I search for several moments for a suitable tool before my eyes rest on what I really need: a sledgehammer.

My hands grip the shaft and for one clear moment, I'm ready to abandon this whole foolish quest. Just leave it alone and go back to bed.

But I can't do that.

I need to know.

I make my way back into the dining room, dragging the heavy sledge behind me. It scrapes the ground with a dull rasp. The pounding of my pulse in my ears is deafening.

Maybe that's why I don't hear the car drive up, or the front door open.

Everything happens so fast. It blurs together and none of it makes sense.

I raise my sledge in both hands, over my head, ready to smash open the statue that may double as a tomb. Ready to prove, for sure, whether I've walked into a trap.

From the doorway, Blackwood yells, "No!"

He rushes toward me. I catch a glint in his eye—fear and fury and aggression. The look a dog gets before it bites.

He runs for me and I turn toward him and I don't know what I'm doing. The sledgehammer falls. Maybe I dropped it. I can't remember.

It falls through the air and collides with a wet thump—the sound of a rotten pumpkin smashed against the curb.

Blackwood crumples.

He doesn't die immediately. His eyes stare up at me, huge and white in the misshapen, bloody mask of his face. They're wide with shock. He starts to say something, but the word is a wet gurgle that dies in his throat. All he can do is blow bubbles of blood from lips in a mouth whose teeth have been smashed in.

The bubble pops, and he's gone.

~*~

I sit on the dining room floor for a long time. I feel numb inside. Too numb to move, or to be afraid. The burning need to know the secret of the statues is gone. I realize I don't *want* to know. It's too late to matter now.

I don't know how long I sit there, my insides quaking, but it's as if time has ceased to make sense. Finally, I struggle to my feet and grab Blackwood's ankles. *I have to do something with the body,* I think, then realize I know exactly what to do.

I drag his body down the hall, trailing a bright smear of blood. I pull it into the studio.

Making the statue isn't so hard.

The instructions are simple to follow. I use the measurements from the sketches he'd done of me. They get me close enough.

Making the statue isn't easy, but the effort calms me. By the time I walk away to allow the concrete to dry, my insides have stilled.

I go into the kitchen, taking care not to look into the dining room. Methodically, I go through the motions of making a sandwich.

I don't get out much.

The voice in my head is so sudden that I jump, as if hearing it aloud.

Even when I have an exhibit, I stay in a hotel. I prefer to deal with everyone over the phone. I can't remember the last person I met face to face.

Nobody even knows his real name, I realize.

Something twists in my gut, but it's not fear.

Nobody will ever notice the difference.

15

Transilience

Every time I open my eyes, I see that the world has changed.

Sometimes the jump is small—a few minutes, hours. I'll wake up and it'll be like I'd only dozed off for a while. Like I'd slipped away into a dream during class and no one saw my chin slump down into my chest, or if I'd nodded off during a movie. But sometimes it seems to jump faster, farther, and I don't know how to make it stop.

When I fell asleep last time, it was springtime. The trees were in bloom, and I could see them from my bedroom window: pink and white blossoms that stood out against rainy gray skies. That night, I opened my window so I could listen to the sound of the toads and crickets, so I could smell the fresh scent of dew and flowers.

When I woke up, it was freezing cold. Snow swirled in an icy spiral outside my window, littering my windowsill with frost. Outside, all the trees were dead, their leaves huddled in piles under drifts of snow. The house was empty and quiet, and it felt like it had been that way for a long time—the way an old attic feels musty and abandoned.

Inside, in my gut, I felt something squirm, and my hand dropped to my belly. And that's when I noticed how large it was, the way it swelled outward like the surface of an inflated balloon.

~*~

I don't know how long it's been since it started. The jumps make it hard to keep time straight—I can't remember how much of *my* time has passed while the world blazes past me. I lose track of the nights, and everything blurs together like the shapes outside the window of a train.

I think, maybe, it began when I started having the dream.

In the dream, I'm a princess. I'm tall and beautiful, with red-gold hair that falls in waves around my shoulders and pale, perfect skin like alabaster—not splotched and pimpled like in real life. I'm wearing a dress of rich gold that brings out the strands of blonde in my hair.

In the dream, something's wrong with me.

I'm sick, or maybe cursed. I'm lying still and cold on a bed, with my hands loosely folded over the blankets. My eyes are closed, the lashes are dark against my cheek. I'm still alive— my chest rises and falls, and my breath makes faint tendrils of fog in the cold room—but my body is like a prison. I see it from above, and because it's a dream, I feel it from the inside, too. There are flowers everywhere, and it makes the room smell cloying and sweet. They're not flowers that someone brought for me; they're flowers that grow here, in this strange cold room, and they grow over the cracks and crevices of the stone wall.

It's strange to have a dream about sleeping, but it's the dream I always have, and now it feels like the only dream I could *ever* have.

There's a prince in my dream, too. He wears armor that gleams like moonlight and the sword on his belt is so long it nearly drags the floor. I think he might be handsome, but I'm not sure; I can never see his face. His features blur together, like they were painted in watercolors that had been mixed too thin.

In the dream, he comes to my bed, and his footsteps sound heavy against the cold stone floor. He takes my hand and kisses it, touching my limp fingertips to his lips before returning my hand, carefully, to my blankets. Then he bends over my face to kiss me, full on the lips. And even though I'm asleep—or paralyzed, or trapped within my body—he parts my lips and presses his tongue against my teeth until they open and let him inside.

And with his kiss, I wake up, and see that the world has changed.

~*~

The first time, the change wasn't so big. It had been a Saturday when I went to sleep, but it was Monday when I awoke. I woke up in my classroom. My face was numb and drool crusted the corners of my mouth. My teacher gave me a stern look. The other kids laughed at me—but I was afraid. I tried to tell my teacher that I didn't know how I'd gotten there. That I didn't remember coming to school, or where I had been for the last two days.

She sent me to the nurse's office. The nurse looked me over and took my temperature and called my mother. I was so tired that I fell asleep in the car, and in the car I had the dream.

When I woke up, everything had changed again.

~*~

I tried to stop it from happening. I lay awake in the dark, trying to keep my eyes open. I'd started by staying awake in the living room, watching movies in the night, but the movies turned strange and nonsensical and stray noises made me jump. My mom came to ask me why I was awake, and I tried to explain to her. I told her about the dream, the time jumps. I told her I was frightened.

She smoothed back the hair from my face and chided me for being afraid. "Talia, go to bed," she said, ushering me toward my room. "You're too old to be frightened of nightmares."

I tried to explain about the time jump. I tried to remind her about the nurse, about how I'd been sent home from school with a fever. She said she didn't know what I was talking about. That I hadn't missed school in months.

So I sat in the darkness of my room and listened to the boughs creak and the cats yowl like babies outside my window. Outside, everything was dark and cold, and I could see only a wash of gray. Inside, the room flickered and shifted, and I was inside myself but standing beside my bed also, and I understood.

Even if I didn't sleep, the change would come and force itself upon me.

~*~

Brittany says that you can get pregnant from kissing. She told me all about it at a sleepover once. I don't know if kisses in dreams count; she never told me if they did. I was afraid to ask. She always liked to talk about boys, and kissing, and other things that I didn't really understand. They made me uncomfortable, but I pretended to like them so that she wouldn't stop inviting me to her house.

Then again, the last time I saw Brittany, I hardly recognized her. She looked older—not just from makeup, but really grown-up. She caught my eye at the mall, once, after a jump, and I had to stare at her for a long time before I recognized her face. She was standing with a group of women whose faces looked half-way familiar, like photos from an old yearbook, and they waved me over and smiled.

They asked me questions about things that didn't make any sense to me, people I didn't know, and I smiled and tried my best to answer, but all the while I could only think: *Who are these people? How do they recognize me? And when did they get so old?*

But now, I'm starting to realize that it wasn't just them who had grown.

The air in the bathroom is cold against my bare skin, and gooseflesh spreads down my arms. My nipples are hard and wrinkled, and my breasts look like they belong to someone else. Actually, everything on my body looks like it belongs to someone else: the swell of my belly, the fine lines around my lips and eyes, the early hints of gray at my temples. I see myself in hints and glimpses, the way you recognize your features in a family photo album, but the whole doesn't seem like me. I stare at myself for a long time, pulling faces in the mirror until I'm satisfied that the face that peers back at me is truly mine.

When I'm finished, I pull a shirt over my head and tug it down, self-consciously, trying to cover the bulge of my stomach. I don't know why I'm bothering. There's no one home; my house is just as empty and cold as the castle in my dreams. That frightens me, but it doesn't frighten me as much as the thing that moves inside of me—the thing in my stomach that's alive, but I don't know how it got there.

I walk back to my bedroom. It's cold, but I don't close the window. The cold air reminds me that I'm awake, that this is real, and I need that right now. But it's meager comfort: The world in the dream is cold and real, too. Maybe *this* is the dream, I think, touching my hand to my stomach. Maybe my life as the princess is the real one.

I climb into my bed and pull the blankets over my head, squeezing my eyes shut. I've never tried to go back to the dream on purpose, but I do it now. It's too cold here—too empty and too lonely—and the thing inside of me frightens me. I want to sleep, and jump time, and when I awaken maybe it will be gone.

Sleep comes, and the dream washes over me, and I fall from one cold, lonely world into another. In my dream, I look young and fragile. It's another image of myself, another reflection I can hardly recognize. I lay inside myself and outside and wait, frightened, for my prince to come.

The room is cold and smells like lilies. The longer I lie there—frozen, immobile, a thing caught in stasis—the more uneasy I become. I came here because I was scared of the life I woke to, but at least there I had choices. Here, I can only lie and wait.

The panic rises in me, like the fear of a caged animal, and I feel my heart thudding against my chest even as I watch the peaceful expression begin to slip from my placid, sleeping face. Outside, my prince begins the slow climb up the stairway, his boots heavy on the stone. Does he visit me every day? Or is this moment repeated, over and over, an infinite loop that stretches out into eternity?

If I never woke up, would I be trapped here forever?

That thought hits me with a sudden crushing force, like I've been buried alive, and I can't stand it. My eyes roll under heavy lids and my fingertips twitch; I struggle to crawl out of my body or force myself to rise. The prince stops outside my door, and my heart lurches in my chest. I force open my eyes, and for a moment everything seems to stop.

Then the world around me dissolves, and I fall back into reality. I'm on the sofa, my neck creaking and sore from sleeping at an awkward angle. An infant lies against my chest, her hands curled in tiny fists. Her lashes are dark against her cheeks, and in her face I see something familiar—another reflection of myself. Carefully, so I don't wake her, I gather her in my arms and rise from my seat.

~*~

Outside, the sun is bright and clear. From the windows, I can see the sun glint off the snow; the first hint of flowers bloom under a blanket of frost. I open the door, feeling the cool air and pale golden light spill over me.

Somewhere, in a faraway kingdom, a prince mourns the death of a cursed princess, and a fairy-tale ends before its prime.

I walk outside, holding my daughter in my arms.

Author's Notes

Thank you for reading. I hope you've enjoyed this journey through birth and childhood, traumatic coming-of-age and monstrous inheritance.

I never set out to write a collection of childhood horrors, but it's a theme I return to often in my work. It's at the heart of my first novel, *The Darkness of Dreamland*, and it's woven through many things I've written in the years since. I realized I had several stories with a similar through-line and, once I went digging through my files, I discovered quite a few more that fit like puzzle pieces, and strange connections, deeper meanings, and surprising overlaps started to emerge.

~*~

Earlier versions of "Beware the Wolves," "Blackwood," and "Transilience" appeared in my debut short story collection of dark fairy-tale re-imaginings, *The Beast in the Bedchamber*, initially published in 2012. It was a Kindle exclusive that is now out of print, so I'm happy to give these stories new life here.

"The Toymaker" was written for *Trust Me*, an anthology about dolls that sometimes tell lies, edited by Josh T. Jordan and published by Ginger Goat Press in 2014.

Acknowledgments

This book is the culmination of many years of work, and something of a time capsule of the people who have helped me get here.

Thanks to Martin Shannon for the stellar cover.

To Josh T. Jordan, who took a chance on me as a newbie author, and to Elford Alley and John Daly, who have been in my corner from the beginning.

To Angel, who's both champion and cheerleader, and all of the crowd at The Bleeding Pen.

And to my husband David, who always indulges and co-signs my flights of fancy.

About the Author

T.L. Bodine writes horror at the intersection of the fantastic and mundane. Her work often deals with themes of grief, survival, monstrosity, and the subtle ways people can destroy each other's lives.

She is the author of several novels, including the survival thriller *Neverest*, the Books of Lazarus trilogy (*River of Souls*, *House of Lazarus* and the upcoming *Cage of Bones*), the dark fantasy *The Darkness of Dreamland*, and the Wattpad-exclusive *The Hound*, which has been optioned for film.

When not writing, she can usually be found watching horror movies, playing story-heavy video games, or experimenting in the kitchen.

She lives in New Mexico with her husband and two small dogs.

Learn more at www.tlbodine.com